T0162637

CROWE'S NEST

SOMETIMES THE "EVERYMAN"
IS THE ONLY MAN FOR THE JOB

E.W. NICKERSON

Order this book online at www.trafford.com
or email orders@trafford.com

Most Trafford titles are also available at major online book retailers.

Author Photo by Betty McDowell

Printed in the United States of America.

ISBN: 978-1-4669-6154-8 (sc)
ISBN: 978-1-4669-6156-2 (hc)
ISBN: 978-1-4669-6155-5 (e)

Library of Congress Control Number: 2012918177

Trafford rev. 10/12/2012

 www.trafford.com

North America & international
toll-free: 1 888 232 4444 (USA & Canada)
phone: 250 383 6864 ♦ fax: 812 355 4082

I would like to thank my wife Judy and my friend Sue Manson for their help, assistance, and direction in helping me with this my third novel.

CHAPTER ONE

SATURDAY NOVEMBER 3ᴿᴰ 1984. 10:05 A.M. OAKVILLE, ONTARIO, CANADA

• • • • • • • •

P at walked into the foyer of the apartment building and looked at the nameplates. The names were in alphabetical order. Under 'C' was 'Crowe, Ed, Apt. 528'. She quickly took a pen from her purse, extracted the paper name slip from under the plastic and wrote on the back—'Crowe's Nest—528'. She slipped it back under the plastic, proud of herself. She picked up the phone and pressed 5-2-8.

"Bon jour," Ed said with a distinctive non-French accent.

"Bon jour yourself," she said. "I didn't realize you spoke French so poorly."

"You'd be surprised at what I can do poorly," he laughed. "Come on up. Tea is ready."

He buzzed her in. She entered the elevator, pressing the button to the fifth floor. As usual she complained inwardly about the height of the button, happy that Ed was not on the fifteenth floor. At just over five feet she didn't need to be reminded that most things were built for a taller stature.

After she knocked, the door opened a few inches and a bunch of flowers were presented through the gap. She took them, smiling at the thoughtfulness. In return she slipped her over-night bag into the room

Ed opened the door wide and welcomed her in. "Only five minutes late. Not bad."

They hugged each other quickly.

"I hope you didn't buy these for me yesterday," Pat smiled, "before you invited me here—assuming I'd accept, that is?"

"Fresh this morning, Pat. Have faith in your old friend." He took the flowers and put them in a vase as she checked out her self-described 'Crowe's Nest'.

She was impressed with his apartment or flat as he called it. It was furnished sparingly with few ornaments. The exception was a collage of photos from Turkey, mostly in and around Ankara, on the wall above the gas fireplace. They were photos that Ed had taken on his trip to Turkey that had resulted in his first consulting role with The British Secret Service—MI6. Integral to that operation, he had visited Canada and met Pat. "Very nice," she said approvingly. "You've done alright for yourself."

"Not bad for a Delayed Pioneer eh?"

She smiled. "Not bad at all. Which room is mine?"

He showed her the guest room. It faced onto Lakeshore Road. She looked out at the view and enjoyed the memories of living in the area. She threw her bag on the bed and turned to him. "You understand this is a sex-free weekend do you?"

He acknowledged the message with a smile and a nod. "It's great to see you, Pat. How about a big hug?"

"Just a hug," she said, walking into his arms. "No dirty stuff!"

They held each other tight for longer than normal, both reluctant to let go. She took great pleasure in being held by her one and only lover even enjoying, but never admitting, that his six foot height gave her comfort. He bent slightly and kissed the top of head. They squeezed each other a little tighter.

"Let me show you the balcony," he said, separating from her. "I'll serve tea in two minutes."

Ed walked her to the balcony and went back inside to pour the tea. It gave Pat the opportunity to recall the first time they had met, just over six months ago in April when he visited Toronto for three days to become 'Canadian'". They didn't hit it off too well at the start. She was running her first operation and he was uncertain of both his role on behalf of MI6, and the risk he was taking in Operation Niagara. After three days of working together they warmed up to each other enough to agree that if Ed ever returned to Toronto they would go on a real date. As it turned out he returned the following weekend battered and bruised from his trip to Turkey. She smiled as she recalled that very quickly they were lovers. She loved him dearly, but knew he would never return the deep feelings she held. It was a situation she was willing to accept. When Ed had visited Ottawa, where Pat now lived, they were again lovers. Such contact was contrary to her departmental rules which they 'bent' by becoming engaged to be married for the shortest of time. She wondered if he still carried the aluminum-foil engagement ring, which they used in their ruse, in his wallet.

Ed carried the tea out to the balcony and placed the tray on the table between then. "I'll be mother," he grinned, and poured.

"Nice view," she said, as they looked over Sixteen Mile Creek as it entered into Lake Ontario.

"I'm very lucky," he agreed. "And I very much acknowledge that I owe this in large part to you."

She waved him off. "Yeah, yeah," she said.

"Look Pat," he said, drinking his tea, "I want you to know I really appreciate your coming to visit me today. It means a lot to me."

She looked at him over her cup. "You're not trying to sweet-talk me into bed are you, Ed?"

He shook his head, smiling. "No. I doubt I have the skill to do that. You have too strong a will for that to happen too easily."

She gave a quick shrug. "You could try!"

He laughed aloud. "Okay, I'll keep that in mind. But for now, why don't you tell me, what you can that is, about your new role in Ottawa."

She put her cup down. "I'm planning on staying until Monday morning if that's okay?"

"Perfect, I don't go into work until twelve noon."

"Yes, I know."

He gave her a sideways look.

"That's part of my job Ed. You're part of my job, that is."

"Really?" He pulled a face. "Are you what they call my handler?"

"Nothing like that. I just keep on top of your general movements. For your safety that is."

"Yikes, I feel a little squirmy about that."

She smiled. "You don't have to. I know your work hours because we helped you find the job, right? And if you left the country, I'd know very quickly where you were." She poured them both more tea. "Hey, I'm here this weekend as a guest, not on the job . . . so to speak."

"Hmm," he mumbled.

"Let me put it this way. If you were running around with a married woman, or a married man for that matter, I wouldn't know. But if you got a DUI ticket, or crossed the US border, I'd find out very quickly."

"And you're telling me this because . . . ?"

"Because we're friends, and friends don't keep things from friends unless they have to. And I don't have to. It's part of the process. What I think London needs to know, I tell them."

"And will you tell London about visiting me this weekend?"

"Absolutely not. This is personal."

He still felt uncomfortable, and it showed.

She reached over and took his hand. "Ed, you asked me what I do in Ottawa. It's one of many things I do. The significant part of my job is monitoring issues of a potential security risk for our representatives across the world. And while I don't want to sound rude, you're not on my top-ten list of security concerns. In fact your name hasn't crossed my desk since you last came back to Canada." She paused. "This doesn't mean I haven't thought about you once or twice."

He squeezed her hand. "Then why don't we go to bed, and discuss what your thoughts about me were?"

She pushed away his hand. "Get a grip. Real sweet-talking that is! About as subtle as a two-by-four across the head."

"It's a start," he said grinning.

She changed the conversation. "Do you have any plans for us tonight?" she asked.

"None. I thought we'd play it carefully. You being dead in these parts that is."

"Yeah, an unfortunate circumstance of Operation Niagara," she nodded. "So can I arrange to take you out tonight?"

"It'll be my pleasure. Where to?"

She winked. "It'll be a surprise. Let me use your phone, and don't listen to my conversation." She went inside and closed the sliding door.

It had been a shock to everyone that Pat's apartment in the Oakville area of greater Toronto had been bombed by the Turkish terror organization PKK. The apartment had, however, been of concern to her superiors and Pat and her cat had left only hours before the blast. Ed had left even later. The Canadian authorities, with approval from the highest level, had issued death certificate's for both Pat Wilson and an unidentified male. While Wilson was not her real name she now used Pat Weston, and the move to Ottawa helped secure her safety.

She returned to the balcony and sat down. "We're being picked up at 5:30 this afternoon. Shirt and tie for you please."

Ed nodded. "So tell me more about your job."

She turned to face him. "Well the good thing, thanks to you; and I do mean *thanks* to you, I am *the* main Ottawa contact on the Brighton Bombing Committee. And even better, I'm a member of the IRA Surveillance Task Force."

"I am impressed." Ed leaned forward and spoke quietly. "So you really do work for CSIS, right?"

"Don't be silly," she said, feigning insult. "I work for Export Development Canada. That's what my business card says, and that's what I do."

"As you say, Miss Wilson, as you say."

"That's Weston. Remember Miss Wilson is dead!"

He smiled. "Of course I remember. It's Miss W. then."

She shrugged, thinking about it. "That'll be fine."

Ed wanted to ask more about the details of her work regarding the IRA, but knew better than to ask. He didn't want to put Pat in the situation of having to claim 'security issues' and neither did he want to know details that put her at risk if he was in any way forced into providing details. The chance of such a situation was slim, of that he was sure, but his short time in 'the trade' had taught him—as Mr. Cooper had so carefully outlined—the less you knew, the less you had to lie about. He was, however, proud of Pat's accomplishments in her new role and pleased that his, albeit accidental, involvement in the IRA Brighton Bombing affair had contributed to her increased responsibilities.

"So tell me something, Pat. Nothing to do with the Brighton Bombing or your actual involvement with the IRA Task Force, but have you studied the history of the IRA?"

"Of course."

"Then give me a thumb-nail sketch of the IRA, where it started and where it is today."

"I don't do thumb-nail sketches," Pat replied. "You either get to hear all I know, or nothing."

Ed sat back in his chair. "Then I'm all ears."

Pat took a deep breath and started. "The Irish Republican Army was a direct descendent from the Irish Republican Brotherhood. You will, of course, recall that it was the Brotherhood that staged the Easter Rising in 1916 and declared a free Irish Republic. Their timing was intentional, but disastrous as it turned out. Britain was at war with Germany, and Germany had given the Brotherhood guns and ammunition. That made the rebellion an act of war and the leaders of the Rising traitors. The result was that they were all killed by firing squad, with no trials or formal legal process. In any event, this eventually led to the IRA becoming, in effect, the representatives for a free, or freer, Ireland. In 1921 the IRA signed the Anglo-Irish Treaty which ended the Irish War of Independence. Essentially the Treaty set up what was to be the Irish Free State, consisting of all of Ireland and still attached to Britain and part of the Commonwealth. Very similar to Canada, New Zealand, and Australia. The Treaty was signed by Winston Churchill and others on behalf of the U.K and Michael Collins as head of the IRA, along with other IRA representatives. But the Treaty was violently opposed by many members of the IRA. The result was fighting between members of the IRA and the Irish people in general in what we know as the Irish Civil War." Pat took a sip of tea. "Want me to carry on?"

"Absolutely. This is really interesting."

"Setting aside the terrible events of the civil war, it ended in 1922 with the establishment of the Irish Free State as basically outlined in the Anglo-Irish Treaty, except that the day it came into effect, the north exercised its right to exclude itself from the Treaty, and Northern Ireland was established. In the south, the IRA was still opposed to any connection with Britain and the fighting has continued ever since. IRA members didn't recognize either the Irish Free State, or Northern Ireland—period. Now there was a great deal of brutality in all of this, especially by the Black and Tans—bloody English!"

"Blimey," Ed managed.

"Blimey indeed," Pat agreed. "Now in 1939 the Republic of Ireland came into effect, but the fighting continued. Then in 1969 things got worse. The IRA split into two separate organizations. The Official IRA, or OIRA, basically ceased fighting and became a political organization; the Worker's Party of Ireland. The Provisional IRA, PIRA, continued fighting, mainly in the north in an effort to return Northern Ireland to the south, so to speak. That, of course, is what we refer to as The Troubles. OIRA ceased to exist as such in the seventies. So when we talk of the IRA today it is really the Provisional wing, but simply known as the IRA. There have been other smaller changes, not important for this discussion, within the IRA, but basically that's the history." Pat grimaced. "Not a pleasant tale to tell."

"Indeed not. So," Ed asked thoughtfully, "my involvement in the Paris activity connected to the IRA resulted in your recent promotions at work?"

As soon as Pat started to reply with a cheeky grin, Ed knew he shouldn't have raised the issue. "Well now, Mr. Crowe, are you asking me if your pretending to have sex with Carolyn Andrews in a grungy hotel in Paris with members of the IRA and some Libyan terrorists listening in from the room next door helped my promotion? And further, Mr. Crowe, are you asking me if your stripping to your underwear in front of the same Carolyn Andrews to answer the door to the said IRA members qualifies as assistance to my promotion?" She raised a hand to stop him from replying. "And finally, Mr. Crowe, are you going to tell me what Carolyn Andrews did or said of you in your state of undress?"

"What one has to do for one's country?" Ed muttered.

"And Miss Andrews reaction?"

Ed shrugged. "I guess if she saw something she'd never seen before, she could have thrown something at it."

"And?"

"She kept her heard covered up by the blanket. Remember she was supposed to be naked."

"Good answer, Ed," Pat laughed. "Besides we shouldn't be talking about our fellow operatives, should we? Especially someone as nice and sweet as Carolyn is."

"Agreed," Ed replied quickly.

"I just bet you do, mister." Pat chuckled. "I just bet you do."

With Carolyn Andrews the love of Ed's life, he wanted to change the direction of the conversation. "But my input still helped your move ahead?"

"Absolutely," she said. "But if you think that's going to get you any special favors you've got another thing coming, young man!"

"Tut, tut, Miss W. you should have greater faith in me. I was going to ask if my minor contribution to your promotion is, in part anyway, the reason that you're taking me out tonight?"

She stood up, taking the advantage to look down at him. "No, I'm taking you out because I like you, nothing to do with business. I told you this is a personal weekend. Now let's go for a drive and you can buy me a Tim Hortons coffee . . . or two."

He stood up, took her hand and raised it to his lips. "As you say, Miss W., and the pleasure will be all mine."

She nodded curtly. "Yes, I think it will."

"So what kind of car did you drive in England?" Pat asked, as they headed out of Oakville.

Ed laughed. "Me afford a car? I couldn't have afforded the insurance, let alone a car. I did drive a moped once, but that was when I worked two jobs and I needed it to get around."

Pat feigned a tear. "We were so poor . . ."

Ed shook his head. "No, I just wanted some extra spending money. I collected insurance premiums every Friday evening and Saturday morning and a moped was the way to go."

"Hard working chap then, were we?"

"Just a bit of extra beer money. Besides I had to keep up with my friend Roy. He had, and has, a pretty good job, plus he has a car. Couldn't let him pay for the petrol too could I?"

"But you can afford a car here okay," Pat said, looking around the interior. "This is a nice whatever-it-is."

"Dodge Mirada, 1981. Second-hand of course, but I like it."

"Pretty good for a recent D.P., I'd say."

"You're all charm, Pat," Ed laughed. "You're all charm."

She nodded her agreement.

They picked up coffees at the closest Tim Hortons and headed into Ontario wine country. The cold nights and declining sunlight hours had turned the trees into a variety of reds and golds.

"This is spectacular," Ed said. "Nothing like this in London."

"Hmm, I wouldn't know," Pat replied thoughtfully, "having never been there."

Ed turned to her, and smiled. "You'd be welcome at my mum's place whenever you want to visit. I mean that."

"I'll keep that in mind," she said, looking out at the colors. "We'll have snow soon."

"I'm looking forward to that. Real snow and lots of it."

She turned and pulled a face. "Tell me that next March."

They reached the top of a hill, pulled into a tourist viewing spot and turned off the car. They sipped their coffees enjoying the view. It was a clear sunny day, with a definite nip in the air.

She pointed north across the lake. "Toronto the Good," she said. The outline of Toronto was clearly visible, set off wonderfully by the CN Tower

He raised his eyebrows, questioning.

"That's what it used to be called," Pat said. "Everything closed on Sundays, men-only beer parlors and you couldn't see the goods at the LCBO. They were all hidden in the back. The government treated everyone like children. God, it was awfully boring."

They finished their coffees and Ed drove home taking the back roads.

When they entered Ed's apartment, Pat walked straight to her bedroom and returned with several sheets of paper.

"Would you like to see a summary of the details of the Brighton bombing to refresh your memory?" she asked, offering the papers to Ed. "Don't worry, nothing Top Secret, just the facts as generally known." Ed took the report and sat at the kitchen table to read it. "I'll make tea, and be mother," Pat added.

Ed opened the report:

Brighton hotel bombing
(IRA, Provisional IRA, Patrick Magee, The Troubles)
NOT FOR RELEASE TO THE PUBLIC

The Brighton hotel bombing occurred at The Grand Hotel in Brighton on October 12th 1984, at 2:54am. It was intended to kill Prime Minister Margaret Thatcher and members of her Cabinet.

Five people died, namely: Sir Anthony Berry, MP; Roberta Wakeman, wife of Parliamentary Treasury Secretary John Wakeman: Lady Muriel Maclean, who was in the room in which the bomb exploded with her husband Sir Donald Maclean; Eric Taylor; and Jeanne Shattock.

Thirty-four people were taken to hospital with a variety of injuries. At the time of the bombing, Prime Minister Thatcher was working on her next day's speech for the Conservative Party conference. She was not injured.

It is estimated that the bomb was 20-30 lb.

The following day the IRA claimed responsibility in a released statement. It read:

> *"Mrs. Thatcher will now realize that Britain cannot occupy our country and torture our prisoners and shoot our people in their streets and get away with it. Today we were unlucky, but remember we only have to be lucky once. You will have to be lucky always. Give Ireland peace and there will be no more war."*

Police are tracing all guests of the hotel in the month prior to the bombing.

End of Report . . . . PAW

Ed put down the report and looked at Pat. "I assume you're PAW?"

"That's me. Any comments; on the report that is?"

"Working on her speech at 3am in the morning! She is some lady."

"She most certainly is," Pat agreed, pouring milk into their cups. "And I can tell you that MI5 is pretty sure that Patrick Magee is the bomber." She poured and brought the cups of tea to the table. "But that is a still not entirely public, so mum's the word."

"Understood," Ed said nodding. He also appreciated that Pat was willing to trust him. He thanked her with a knowing smile. "Speaking of mums, I can tell you something about the Grand Hotel, if you're interested."

"Please do." Pat said, now impressed.

"It is a very large and fancy hotel, very fancy. When my mum and I used to sit on the beach at Brighton, we always sat in front of the Grand Hotel . . . pretending we were residents of the hotel. Rather posh, like."

Pat laughed. "Is this a 'we-were-so-poor' story?"

Ed shook his head, thinking back to those days with his mum. "Not at all. Mum always said 'we had everything, except money'. Not such a bad philosophy, eh?"

It wasn't often that Pat felt she had said the wrong thing to Ed, but she had that thought now. "Look I'm sorry, I didn't mean to . . . you know."

"No need to apologize, Pat. When you meet my mum, you'll understand where her heart is. She'll like you, for sure."

"Really?" Pat asked. "Well I am chuffed. Why do you think that?"

Ed toasted her with his cup of tea. "Because you're smart, sharp as a whip, and not afraid to express your opinion."

Pat gave him a sideways look. "Are you sure that's intended as a compliment?"

"Absolutely," Ed said, moving to pour more tea. "That's why I like you too."

Pat grinned. "Okay, I believe you!"

• • • • • • • •

Paris, France

The two men moved closer to each other across the restaurant table.

"She's into the booze again," said the larger man, motioning with his head to a lady at another table. He had a strong Irish accent. "She's the one. Let's keep our eye on her."

The second man nodded his understanding.

CHAPTER TWO

THAT EVENING IN OAKVILLE

• • • ● ● ● •

B y twenty past five they were dressed and ready to go. Pat was wearing a black business suit with a buttoned top and a knee-length skirt.

"You look very nice, Pat," Ed said, standing as she came out of her bedroom.

"Do you like it?" she asked, turning to show it off.

"Very nice. Professional. Sexy even." Ed admired her again. "Can I get a hug?"

"No!"

"Why not?"

"You know why not."

"Remind me again."

"Because," she said firmly, "you'll put your hand under my top. You'll enjoy that too much . . . and so would I. So the answer is no."

He walked closer to her. "Trust me," he said.

She nodded her head knowingly as she walked into his arms.

His hands went under the back of her top and he spread them across the small of her back. To make the point, he slid his hands under her bra strap.

She held him tight, holding her face against his chest. "Thanks. That does feel nice. Even if you lied abut it."

He bent his head and kissed the top of her head. "You smell nice," he said quietly, "and I love your new hair style, especially the fringe."

She looked up at him. "Sometimes, just sometimes, you say such the nicest things, Ed. But I should tell you the next time you say this to a Canadian girl in your arms, we call them bangs." She squeezed him extra hard. "And please don't say anything naughty about liking my bangs, okay."

"It never crossed my mind," he lied.

They separated. She adjusted her top, checked her hair and lipstick in the mirror and tilted her head to the door. "Let's go. I've got a full evening planned for us."

He opened the door slightly, taking the opportunity to kiss her forehead as he did. "I'm looking forward to this evening. It's great spending it with you."

She smiled up at him, straightened her back in order to reduce the difference in their height, and led them to the elevator.

As they entered the limousine the driver handed Pat a small envelope. She slipped it into her purse, not responding to Ed's questioning look. They both sat in the rear seat in order to enjoy the ride. It wasn't long before Ed realized they were heading to downtown Toronto. The QEW was still busy in the other direction as commuters headed home from downtown shopping.

Ed turned to face Pat. "Do you realize it was only five months ago we were doing this run for Operation Niagara; me as your guest and you as the boss?"

"It never crossed my mind," Pat lied. "And I'm still the boss."

"I thought you said . . ." but she interrupted.

"I'm the boss because I'm at a more senior level than you, not your boss, boss."

He accepted that. "Okay you're the boss. Just keep that in mind if I charge you with sexual harassment."

"In your dreams, Edwin William Crowe."

"Maybe so," he mused. "Just maybe so."

They looked at each other and smiled. They turned their minds and their conversation to the scenes of the city around them as the limousine drove smoothly through the evening traffic.

The limousine pulled up in front of the Royal York Hotel. Pat and Ed waited for the driver to open the door for them. The hotel was one of Toronto's finest. Twenty years earlier it had been the largest building for miles around, but was now dwarfed by office towers—mostly head offices for the country's largest banks. However the hotel's mystique and glamour was still very much in place, and this was especially obvious as they walked into the lobby area.

"Are we eating here?" Ed asked.

"Indeed we are, eh!" Pat answered, taking Ed's arm and steering him through the hotel lobby.

The lobby was as opulent as Ed had recalled it when he had first seen it in May, five months earlier. Many of the men around the massive lobby were wearing tuxedos, and there was a considerable expanse, and expense, of jewellery on the ladies with them.

Pat pulled on Ed's arm and leaned into him. "I left my diamonds in Ottawa," she chuckled.

"You're cute," Ed said, winking down to her. "I like you."

Pat steered them to the entrance of *The Acadian Room,* the hotel's finest restaurant. They let go of each other as they reached the maitre d'.

"Reservation for Crowe," Pat said, speaking somewhat formally. "I believe our Executive Assistant requested a special table?"

The maitre d' bowed courteously. "Yes, she did madam. Please follow me."

Pat jabbed Ed in the ribs quickly with her elbow as they walked slowly toward their table. "Stick with me kid," she whispered. "Places to go, things to see."

Pat ordered a bottle of wine and they chatted about the weather, with Pat trying to convince Ed that lots of snow is not always a good thing. When the wine arrived Pat sniffed the cork, held the glass to her nose, and then tasted it slowly. She nodded to the waiter, who poured them a glass each and silently left them to themselves.

"So what do you search for in testing the wine?" Ed asked politely.

Pat leaned forward. "I have no idea. As long as it tastes okay, then I give the man the nod."

Ed smiled. "And if it didn't taste okay?"

"Oh God," she groaned, "I don't know what I'd do. Probably ask the waiter to taste the wine, and see what he says."

They clinked glasses gently and each took a sip.

"Well?" she asked.

Ed swirled the wine across his palate. "Very nice," he agreed. "My hostess is classy, quite the most beautiful lady in the room, and a pleasure to be with." He raised his glass to toast her.

"Thank you, Ed," Pat said, picking up her menu. "I do believe you're making me blush." She hid her face behind the menu.

They selected their meals and ordered.

"So how old are you, Pat?" Ed asked as they finished their dessert.

"You can't ask me that," she said. "You don't ask a lady her age. Didn't they teach you any manners in England?"

Ed chuckled. "Well I wouldn't ask a middle-aged lady her age, but you're most certainly not that."

"Well, I'm glad you've figured that out. Besides I'm younger than you. Let's leave it at that."

"Okay, when is your birthday?"

She took a sip of her wine. "Why do you ask?"

"So I know when to phone and wish you a happy birthday. Nothing tricky here."

She looked squarely him in the eyes. "August 24th. So is that the next time you're going to speak to me?"

Ed shook his head. "No, Pat. We're going boating in June, remember?"

She smiled and inwardly was comforted. "Yes, of course we are. I'm looking forward to that very much."

"So am I."

She wagged a finger at him. "Remember, no hanky panky!"

"It never crossed my mind," he lied.

After she paid the bill, she withdrew the small envelope from her purse. "This evening's main event," she said. "Two tickets to see *Cats*."

Ed narrowed his eyes. "Cats?"

"The musical, you dummy. Haven't you ever heard of *Cats*? Oh, for God's sake. Who did I ask out for a date?"

Ed looked around leaned forward and began quietly singing, *Memory. All alone in the moonlight . . .*

15

Pat applauded out loud; not caring about the many eyes turned their way. "Oh, Ed, that's wonderful." She jumped up from her chair and reached for his hand. "Let's go!"

It was a quick cab ride to the Elgin Theatre on Yonge St. Ed tried to pay, but Pat insisted. The theatregoers were excited about the performance they were about to see. It was easy to absorb the excitement, which they both did enthusiastically. The theatre had recently undergone major renovations and it was wonderfully decorated. This production of Cats was the first performance at the new theatre. They took their seats early: eighth row—centre.

"I am impressed," Ed said, looking around.

"I'll thank my father for you," Pat said, beaming with excitement.

"Maybe I can do it myself sometime?" Ed smiled.

"Maybe," Pat replied, waving off the discussion.

The lights dimmed, and the music started. Pat turned to face the stage, grinning, Ed thought appropriately, like the cat that had just caught a mouse.

The limousine was waiting for them as the audience streamed out of the theatre. The show had been wonderfully accepted with four curtain calls. All had been enchanted with the music and the dancing. Several ladies were crying, recalling the final song. Pat was overjoyed and couldn't, or wouldn't, stop talking about how Bustopher Jones was just like her cat Robin. Ed indicated his favourite cat was the Siamese.

"You mean the slim, tall, rather busty cat do you?" Pat asked.

"Whatever. She just seemed to have a nice personality." He grinned.

"Men," she muttered.

The thirty-five minute drive to Ed's apartment in Oakville seemed more like five minutes. Pat quickly paid the driver, and holding Ed's hand they made it up to his apartment without waking anyone with their singing.

Ed poured them a glass of wine. They sat looking over the balcony across Lake Ontario. There was not a cloud to be seen and a huge hunter's moon seemed to own the sky.

"Thank you for inviting me down this weekend, Ed," Pat said, sipping her wine. "I owe you one."

"You owe me nothing Miss W., except, perhaps, a quick kiss goodnight."

She handed him her *Cats* programme. "Maybe the Siamese will give you a kiss goodnight?"

He opened the programme to see the photos of the cast. "She would still be my second choice."

"You're too smooth," she commented, sliding her now empty glass across the table. "More wine please."

He topped up their wine. They turned back to the moon.

"You seem to be in deep thought," Ed commented.

"I am." She didn't expand.

"Okay, I'll take the bait. What great worldly question are you contemplating?"

She chewed on her lips in thought. "I'm wondering how I can manipulate the process of kissing you goodnight without ending up in bed with you."

"Hmm, that is a deep and dark question," he agreed. "May I offer you a suggestion?"

"You? You're the problem, not the answer!"

"Hear me out at least."

She waved him on with a flick of her hand.

"So, I kiss you goodnight at your bedroom door. I put my hands up your top as I did earlier, and perhaps even unhook your bra."

"Oh God."

"Then I leave you to go to bed, and I go to my room. On the way . . ."

"Ah, here's the rub!"

"On the way," he repeated, "I take your engagement ring out of my wallet, and leave it here on the kitchen table. If you . . ."

"If I can't stand the thought of your not making love to me," she interrupted, "I pick up the ring on the way to your bedroom and beg for you to make mad passionate love to me. Correct?"

"Well I wouldn't exactly use that phrasing, but yes you would visit my bed chamber and I would then do my best to seduce you."

She took a sip of her wine, looking at him over the glass. "One day, Edwin," she started, lowering her glass, "I'm going to meet your mother and tell her all about you. Tell her how you treat me with such respect and honour, and in spite of that, I end up sleeping with you. Tell her how nice a person you are, yet you had no remorse in shooting two men and kicking a young man in his 'private parts'. Tell her that when your country needed you most, you had to take a pee and almost got yourself killed in doing so." She paused for effect. "So what would your mother think of that?"

Ed pulled a face. "Not very flattering when you put it like that is it? Could you pass on the 'peeing' part? She'd give me heck if she knew I was peeing against a building."

Pat rolled her eyes. "Okay, kiss me goodnight for God's sake. But since I'm still the boss, I've got first dibs on the shower in the morning."

They kissed goodnight as Ed had suggested, and he went to his bedroom leaving the aluminium-foil engagement ring on the kitchen table.

CHAPTER THREE

SUNDAY NOVEMBER 4ᵀᴴ, 1984

• • • • • • •

E d sat up in bed. It was 7:35 and he could hear Pat moving about in the apartment. He decided to let her finish everything she was doing. He wanted her to feel entirely at home. Although he was tempted to walk out of his room naked; he thought better of it. There was a knock on his door.

"Are you awake in there?" Pat called through the door.

"Awake and ready to go, boss."

"Are you decent?"

He smiled. "As decent as it gets."

The door opened and Pat entered with a cup of tea and the newspaper.

"Don't get used to this," she said. "I've been up for hours."

He took the tea and paper.

"You look lovely this morning," he said, admiring her dress that showed off her slim figure well.

"It was a birthday gift," she said, checking the buttons on the front.

"From an admirer?"

She gave him a look. "Don't be rude. I wouldn't take dresses as a gift from a man friend—as if there is one. It's from my mother."

"Well it looks very nice on you. Why don't you come over here and let me feel it?"

"Ha! Are you kidding? I can't trust you as far as I can throw you." She walked toward the door.

He patted the bed next to him. "Trust me."

She walked over and sat on the bed. He took her hand, raised it to his lips and kissed it gently.

"What would you like to do today, Pat? Your wish is my command."

She took her hand back and brushed away a speck of dust from her dress that wasn't there.

"You know damn well what I want to do, Ed, but it's not going to happen. The ring is still on the kitchen table, and it's going to stay there." She swallowed hard, and then managed a smile. "So instead, I'd like you to take me to Niagara Falls. I want you to take me to all of the tourists' spots, especially the tacky ones. I want you to spoil me rotten, and when we come back I want you to make me a nice Sunday meal. How's that sound?"

"Your wish is my command! Now if you'd leave my bedroom, I'll get up and start moving."

She surprised herself, and Ed, by leaning forward and kissing him fully and hard on his lips. He kept his arms at his sides, wanting desperately to pull her into him. She stood up and left the room, closing the door as she left.

"Ten minutes!" she called back. "Be ready to leave in ten minutes."

Twenty minutes later they were on the QEW heading to Niagara Falls. They each had a Tim Hortons coffee, and Pat was flipping through Ed's bird book.

"Any new birds lately?" she asked.

"Quite a few, yes." He took a sip of his coffee.

"Do they all have wings, these new birds of yours?"

He smiled sideways at her. "They all have wings and beaks."

She nodded. "Good."

She flipped to page 190 of the book. "So what can you tell me about Flickers?"

"Members of the Woodpecker family. Yellow-Shafted and Red-Shafted. The male of the Red-Shafted has a red moustache, not black like the Yellow-Shafted."

Pat closed the book. "Very good. You do know your birds."

20

"And they don't get any Woodpeckers in Australia. Did you know that?"

"Now how do you that?" she laughed.

"It's in the book," he replied.

"So what do you do, read the bird book like a novel? Don't get out much do you?"

"I'm here with you, aren't I? Can't beat that."

She shook her head and laughed. "Well I'm glad I got you out and about. I'd hate to think you'd be reading your bird book on your balcony if I weren't here."

He shrugged. "I'd be doing something with birds."

She hit his arm with the book, and decided to change the subject.

"So tell me something about yourself I don't know," Pat asked, turning in her seat to face him.

He took a sip of his coffee and thought for a moment. "Well I'd like to kiss you for one."

"I think I already know that. And keep it about you, not me."

He thought about her question. "I wish I had gone to college or university."

"Yes, I can understand that," she said. "You would have enjoyed the learning experience. You seem to absorb all sorts of useless information. Yes, you'd have done well."

He looked sideways to see if she was being smart, but she looked serious.

"And what about you," Ed asked.

"I thought about being a doctor."

"Wow. And?"

"It takes too long, costs too much money, and you have to deal with old sick people. I decided that wasn't for me."

"So instead you're a lowly civil servant working tirelessly in Export Development Canada, helping companies sell their products around the world."

"Yep, it's all quite boring. Been killed once, and like a good feline eight more lives to go."

"And all the while watching over your friend from Oakville?"

She nodded and took a drink of her coffee. She wanted to expand it to very good friend, ex-fiancé, ex-lover, the one man she loved—but she didn't.

They arrived at Niagara Falls and started their tour at a local restaurant in order to grab a quick snack. They then walked to Louis Tussaud's waxworks, spent some time with The Scarecrow, The Cowardly Lion and with the other members on the Wizard of Oz crew. Pat insisted of a photo of her with Humphrey Bogart. Then they were off to Ripley's Believe it or Not, most of which seemed too bizarre to be true. Ed lived up to spoiling Pat, taking as many photos of her as she would allow; many of which she would not want her friends to see.

They had lunch at the top of the Skylon Tower, 775 feet above the city. The view was spectacular allowing them excellent photos of both the American and the Canadian Horseshoe Falls, as the restaurant revolved 360 degrees each hour.

"You know, Ed," Pat said enthusiastically, "I've visited The Falls many, many times, but this has to be one of the best times. You're a terrific host."

"It really is my pleasure, Pat." He laughed, recalling the first time they had visited together. In preparation for Operation Niagara Pat had arranged for the limo driver to rush them out to Niagara Falls to have a photo of Ed taken with The Falls in the background, which he carried to Turkey as part of his 'proof' that he was Canadian. It was obvious to all from his accent that he was born British.

"Right," she agreed, "and we dated the photo one year earlier. Well it worked, right?"

"It absolutely did. You did a super job of turning me into a Canadian in three days. Come on," he said standing, "lots to see yet."

By 3 p.m. they were both exhausted from walking the hills of the town.

"Where to now?" Ed asked as they pulled out of the parking lot.

"You're going to treat me to a nice hot cup of tea in the tea shop in Niagara-on-the-Lake. If you're up to it that is?"

"Just show me the way, young lady."

The drive took half an hour, including a quick stop at Queenston Heights where Pat reminded Ed again that this was where Canada had beaten the Americans in the War of 1812.

"Sure General Brock was British," she added a tad sarcastically, "but then we've let Brits into Canada for a long time. Still do!"

"And I'm glad you do," Ed smiled.

Ed held Pat's hand as they walked through the shops in the small village of Niagara-on-the-Lake. In addition to just wanting to hold her hand, it also allowed him to pull her past the several shoe shops along the main street. Although it was a cool November day, there were still many tourists—mostly from the U.S. It continued to intrigue Ed that the accents of the American tourists were noticeably different from Canadian accents, in spite of the short distance they all lived from the 'world's longest un-guarded border'. Pat rebuffed the comment, commenting that only Ed had a real accent.

The cup of English Breakfast tea was piping hot and comforting at the 'Olde English Tea Shoppe'. They people-watched, saying little, and after paying the bill, walked to the car. They enjoyed the view and spoke sparingly as they drove home. It was only after a while that Ed noticed that Pat had fallen asleep. He reached over and took her hand. Without opening an eye she smiled, lifted his hand to kiss it, and fell gently back to sleep. He held onto her hand until he eased the car off the QEW and entered the busier streets of Oakville.

They agreed on a pizza for supper-pepperoni and mushroom. Red and green peppers on Pat's side, extra cheese on Ed's.

"I'm going to change out of this dress," Pat said, walking to her bedroom.

"Need any help?" Ed asked quickly, peeling the mushrooms.

"I think I can manage," she called back as she closed the bedroom door.

Ed put on some music, selecting popular classical.

Pat's door opened. The top two buttons of here dress were undone. "I think I need some help in undressing," she said quietly.

"Pat, are you sure? I, er, we . . ."

"And bring the ring please, Ed." She was smiling comfortably.

He picked up the flattened aluminium-foil ring and entered Pat's bedroom. She held out her left hand and he slid the ring onto her ring finger.

"I want you to undress me, Ed," she said, looking up at him. "I want us to make love and not feel guilty in any way." He nodded, pulling her toward him and holding her tight. Taking her hands, he walked to the bed, sat on the edge and had her stand in front of him. He slowly unbuttoned her dress, holding it apart as he did. Her breasts were heaving slightly in her black bra and her ripe nipples showed through the lace. She slid the dress off her shoulders and stepped out of it.

"You have lovely breasts." Ed said, looking up at her.

"Kiss them, Ed."

He reached behind her, unclipped her bra, and removed it slowly. He dropped it on top of her dress and then hungrily sucked on her breasts, moving from nipple to nipple as she directed his head. She groaned in delight as he reached behind her, slid his hands under her panties and squeezed her cheeks.

She pulled him up by his head and began undressing him, kissing and licking him as she slowly removed his clothes. When only his under-shorts were left, she dropped to her knees. Removing his shorts carefully from his erection, she kissed the head of his cock then slowly moved her mouth over him to take in as much as she could. He groaned in pleasure, pushing her onto him until he could feel the back of her mouth. With his cock in her mouth, she looked up smiling.

They moved onto the bed. Both naked, they lay in each other's arms. He gently moved her onto her back, put a pillow under her lower back and started kissing her breasts. Slowly he moved down kissing her, licking her. When he reached her now warm and moist area, she raised her body in anticipation and he thrust his tongue into her. She tried to hold back her scream but couldn't. Her response had him seek deeper into her. She finally pulled his head up, moving his lips back to her nipples.

"I want you in me now," she managed. "Please come in me, Ed. I want to feel you come in me."

He entered her, moving slowly at first. Gradually, carefully he moved faster, holding her breasts, squeezing her nipples. She opened her eyes briefly, smiled and mouthed 'I love you'. He moved quicker now, waiting for her to climax. She held out as best she could, never wanting this to end. As she climaxed, he gave her three hard thrusts and emptied himself into her. He continued thrusting as long as he could, and only left her as she pulled him down by her side.

"Relax, Ed," she smiled. "That was wonderful. I felt you come in me. It was lovely. I asked you to spoil me today, and you certainly accomplished that. Especially just now."

He moved to lie on his side, resting his head on his arm. "You're amazing, Pat." He moved his hand onto her breast and gently touched her nipple. He squeezed her breast hard and moved his mouth over her nipple.

"Slow down now," she said, gently pulling his head away. "It's time for pizza and a glass of wine."

He leant over and kissed her forehead. "Your wish. My command."

Covering herself up with a sheet, she watched him dress and leave for the kitchen. Looking at the ring, she shook her head. "You're a trouble-maker you are. I wonder if I can sue Alcan for sexual assault."

"That was an all-round wonderful day," Pat said, finishing her pizza and sipping on her wine.

"Wonderful two days," Ed added. "What's the story for tomorrow?"

"I get picked up at 10 a.m. Not a problem?"

"Not at all." he took a sip of his wine, looked at her and grinned. "Do you know what day it is tomorrow?"

She looked at him sideways, wondering what the trick was. "It's Monday, November 5th 1984, in the year of our Lord."

"And?"

She shrugged. "Is this some funny English thing about cricket or something?"

"It has to do with religion and politics"

"What doesn't nowadays? Give me a clue."

"1605."

Pat closed her eyes, deep in thought. "The only thing I know about 1605, the year that is, is there were three Popes for the year. Two died. That's religion, not sure about politics."

Ed's jaw dropped. "Good lord, if you'll excuse the pun, but how would you know that?"

Pat smiled, knowing that she had pulled one on him. "You're not the only one to have trivial data stored away in their grey cells. Was that part of the answer?"

"I don't know. You've got me confused. It may be part of the answer."

Pat punched the air with her fist. "The confused Mr. Crowe: my weekend is complete! More wine please." She couldn't have hidden her smile even if she wanted to: and she certainly didn't want to.

He poured them both some more wine, and rubbed his chin in deep thought.

"Cat got your tongue?" Pat quipped.

"One more hint," Ed said. "It was named after a bloke. A bad bloke, but a very religious bloke, who . . ."

Pat closed her eyes to think. Ed assumed he had won, but she opened them with a Cheshire-cat-like grin and a snap of her fingers. "Guy Fawkes—went by Guido actually—the gunpowder plot. He tried to blow up the Houses of Parliament. Actually his goal was to kill King James 1st who was Protestant, while the plotters were Catholic." She took a deep breath of success. "I'm right aren't I?"

Ed stood and bowed. "The lady wins the top prize."

"Which is?" she asked cautiously.

"A night in bed with yours truly," he announced.

"Big deal," she huffed. "What's second prize, a cold shower? I'll take second prize."

"Second prize is having to listen to the way the English celebrate Guy Fawkes Night, or Bonfire Night as it is known."

She took an extra large sip of wine. "Go on then, I'll take second prize. I have no doubt it will last longer and be more interesting."

He pulled a long face. "You can be mean, young lady, very mean. But," he continued merrily, "let me expand on one of the idiosyncrasies, eccentricities and foibles of Jolly Old England, or swinging England . . ."

"Or nearly bankrupt England," Pat interrupted

"Very, very mean."

She toasted his comment, and waved him on to proceed.

Ed outlined the basic story of Bonfire Night in England, ignoring Pat's overt yawning and pinching herself to stay awake.

"So you begged at a bus stop," Pat queried, "by asking for 'a penny for the guy'?"

"Not exactly begging, but close I suppose."

"So then you take all of this ill-gotten money, buy fireworks and scare the hell out of all the dogs and cats in England?"

"No. People kept their pets in on Bonfire Night. We'd have a bonfire, throw on the guy, light a few fireworks, and call it quits. Heck in real life they tortured him and he was then drawn and quartered."

"And how do you intend to celebrate Guy Fawkes Night tomorrow?"

"Well," Ed said winking, "I thought I could give you your own personal fireworks display tomorrow morning."

She rolled her eyes, and slid her glass toward him. "More wine please."

They cleaned up the dishes, both yawning after a long eventful day.

"I'd like to sleep alone tonight, Ed," Pat said, holding his hands. "I really need some sleep."

"Okay," Ed said, kissing her forehead. "Can I pop in tomorrow morning?"

"Pop in?"

"Sorry, bad choice of words. Can I join you in bed tomorrow morning? I'll bring the tea."

She smiled. "Sure, see you tomorrow with a nice cuppa, eh?"

They kissed gently and went separately to their bedrooms.

CHAPTER FOUR

MONDAY, NOVEMBER 5TH 1984

• • • • • • •

E d rapped gently on Pat's bedroom door. Hearing no response he opened it and entered. Pat was still asleep, purring more than snoring. Ed went back to the kitchen and carried their two cups of tea to her bed. Putting them on the night table, he quietly sat on the edge of her bed. He leaned over and kissed her cheek.

"Good morning, sleeping beauty," he whispered.

Pat woke, turned on her back and pulled the sheet up to her neck. "Good morning, Ed. Please do me a favour. Go back to your room, count to one hundred and then come back in to see me. I need to freshen up."

He did as she asked. When he returned Pat was sitting up drinking her tea. Her hair was brushed and her face was fresh and cheery. She was naked.

"Nice cuppa," she said, raising her cup of tea.

He put his cup down, removed his under shorts, and slid in beside her. She moved over to give him room.

"You smell nice," he said, kissing the side of her neck.

"Thanks, so do you." She smiled at him. More of a grin, he thought.

"Everything okay?" he asked.

"I'd like to ask you a favour," she said nervously. He nodded her to continue. "I'd like you to make me come by . . . you know." She reached up and touched his tongue.

"I'd like that," he said, moving his hand over her breast.

"Then I want you to come in my mouth," she added with a smile.

He moved down on her, holding his arms under her legs and holding each breast. She laid back with her hands on his head for encouragement. He worked with her movements, and when she was ready he moved his hand to her clitoris and rubbed gently. "Don't stop, don't stop, don't stop," she begged, squeezing his head in delight as she climaxed.

"Stop, stop," she groaned, pulling him up to her. She clung on to him never wanting let go. He gently kissed her lips, her chin, her eyes, and her forehead.

"I think you came nicely," he said, as she opened her eyes. She nodded, still feeling the warmth inside her.

"Never better," she managed. "I want you to make love to my mouth, Ed. I want you to feel as wonderful as I do now."

She sat up with her back against the wall. Ed straddled her. She held his cock with both hands kissing and licking it, gently at first and then faster and stronger. She leaned back and he moved slowly in and out of her mouth. She reached behind to hold his cheeks, encouraging him to enter her deeply. When he exploded in her mouth she hummed with delight, encouraging him to continue. Exhausted, he collapsed beside her sweat running down his chest.

"Did I tell you," she smiled, "that I've told my mother I have a lover? Not a boyfriend, a lover."

"You didn't?" he asked, his surprise obvious.

"Oh, I did. She doesn't know your name or who you are. Although I did tell her you're British."

"English!"

"Whatever."

"That's nice—I suppose. Why did you tell her?"

"Because I wanted her to know that I've had sex, with you that is. I know she was worried that the way my life was going, it would never happen."

"You surely don't tell her . . . ?"

"What we do? Of course not! I don't tell her how much I enjoy it either. She is my mother!"

"Well when, or if, you meet my mother, I can assure you she won't know our relationship."

"And I'm sure she doesn't think you're a virgin either." She laughed. "Okay end of discussion. I just wanted you to know. What's for breakfast?"

They ate a slow breakfast; discussing the arrangements for the boat cruise they were planning in June. They agreed it would be better for Ed to make his way to Ottawa, and they would cruise leisurely via the Rideau Canal to Kingston and then along the lake to Oakville. Pat would be in charge of bookings, while Ed would be in charge of food and drinks.

Pat removed the ring from her left hand. "I'll see you in June then. It's ten to ten, I gotta go."

Ed took the ring and held it in front of him. "Should I bring this along? I don't want to assume anything."

Pat shrugged with a bit of a smile. "I thought you carried it in your wallet?"

"I do."

"Then leave it in your wallet. One never knows!"

He slowly and deliberately placed the ring back in his wallet.

They collected Pat's bag and he walked her to the door.

"This is fine," she said, kissing him on his cheek.

He pulled her to him and they held each other tight. He opened the door and she walked to the elevator.

"Say 'Hi' to Robin for me," Ed called out.

Pat nodded, but did not look back.

CHAPTER FIVE

PARIS, FRANCE
FRIDAY, DECEMBER 21ST 1984

• • • • • • •

"Terry, for God's sake you're talking way too loud and saying way too much. Sober up and shut up!"

Terry could barely keep her friend Susan in focus. "Mishh Costar," Terry slurred as her head rolled to help keep her focus, "I'm just saying it was a sexy sithuation." She grinned widely and finished off her eighth glass of wine. "Sexy lady is our Carolyn, yeah? And that Mr. Crowe; blooming good! He's for me."

"This is no way to celebrate Christmas, Terry. Come on, let's go," Susan stood, ordering the bill from the now nervous waiter. The bill was ready; Terry had been cut-off; to the great pleasure of the locals sitting close to her table. The waiter delivered the bill and took the money handed by Susan. He had no intention of delivering any change, but simply stood and watched as Susan guided Terry through the tables to the exit.

"Damn English," said a man with a strong Irish accent, "never could hold their drinks." The Parisians that spoke English were only too happy to agree, and those that didn't speak English understood the message from its tone. Everyone in the small bar just off Montmartre was happy to see 'le drunk Anglaise lady' leave them in peace.

The Irishman acknowledged the positive feedback he received with a smile and a wave. He then turned to his friend with a serious look, and spoke in a whisper. "Well now, wasn't that interesting?"

His friend nodded. "Let's drink to that, Paddy my boy. Let's drink to that for sure."

• • • ● ●● • •

Her head was thumping like never before. The bed she was in was wet from her sweat. She was naked. The clock by the bed, not her bed, showed ten o'clock. Rolling over she immediately realized that she was in Susan's flat; in Susan's bed. To make matters worse, Susan was standing by the bed with a cup of tea and a look of total disgust.

"What happened?" Terry managed to ask, reaching for the tea which was now only lukewarm. She drank it in one swallow.

"You made a complete arse of yourself. And if that wasn't bad enough you felt you had to tell the world or at least everyone in the bar, just a few things that you shouldn't have. When we got here you talked to Ralph on the big white telephone—except you missed. But I cleaned it up." She took the cup from Terry, and then sat on the bed. "You're in trouble, girlie, big trouble."

Terry tried hard to remember, but couldn't remember what she had said that would get her into trouble. But she knew Susan Costar was a friend and an honest friend. She took a breath. "Tell me everything. Then tell me what I should do."

Susan stood. "Get dressed and I'll make some more tea, strong tea. Then I'll go over everything I know over breakfast. Fried sausages, fried eggs, fried bread, the works."

Terry covered her mouth and ran. She made it the toilet bowl just in time to vomit for the third time since her friend had half carried her into the flat the night before. "Thanks, friend!" she called out flushing the toilet. She kept her head close to the bowl; just in case. "Never again," she muttered, "never again."

Susan entered the bathroom and covered Terry's naked body with a night gown and patted her on the back. "Tea's ready, hot and sweet."

Seated at the kitchen table and sipping their tea, Susan outlined the story as she knew it from the night before. "So by the time I got to the bar, you were already—what's the expression, past your prime? You were chatting away with a couple of blokes, all three of you having a fine old time. You were mumbling away telling them that you were taking the Mickey."

Terry groaned, hoping for the best. "Were they at least good looking?"

"That wasn't the point, Terry. They were Irish. They *were* micks."

Terry hid her face in her hands and started crying, quietly at first and then bursting into tears. "Oh shit, oh bloody shit! What the hell have I done?" She looked up into her friends eyes, searching for help. "I'm dead. I'm gone. I'm . . . Christ I don't know what I am."

Susan leaned over and touched her hand. "Mind your language now. You're still a Cambridge Uni lady." She paused, allowing time for Terry to calm down. "Here's what we do Terry. You get cleaned up here. We'll go to your place get you in some better, more appropriate clothes, and then we'll phone—I'll phone—the ambassador and ask him to meet us at the embassy. He won't be happy. He's due to fly to London tomorrow for the hols. When he gets there, you'll immediately offer him your letter of resignation and then we'll explain what happened, as least as best we can." She squeezed Terry's hand. "Here's the point, Terry, and this is important. The letter of resignation will be a one-sentence letter. No explanation, no details. And he must read it before you tell the story."

Terry nodded. She understood. "He'll accept it, for sure."

Susan shrugged. "Maybe. Maybe not. But if you tell the story first and then offer the letter, then for sure you're gone. Men work that way. Get their sympathy, and then give them the bad news. It usually works. Let's wait and see."

"You know what the worst part of this will be?" Terry asked, wiping her eyes. "Carolyn's an Oxford type. I'll never live it down!"

Mustering as much humour out of the situation as was possible, they continued with Terry's Christmas from hell.

CHAPTER SIX

FRIDAY MARCH 15TH 1985

• • • • • • •

K aren welcomed Ed to The Queen's Head by having his beer ready as he reached the bar. It was cold and damp outside and the warmth of the pub was welcoming enough. Beer freshly poured as you reached the bar was for regulars only. Ed was now a Friday night regular, although he might drop in from time to time for special occasions—like when he was thirsty—and welcomed friendly chatter with the staff or the other regulars.

"It's cold out there," he said, raising his glass to drink.

"It's March, it's Canada," Karen said. "It's what we do."

Ed was now just about fed-up with his first winter in Canada. It had been long, cold, and snowy. He had thrilled at the white Christmas when his mother had visited, enjoyed all of the lights on the outside of houses. He had even strung a line of lights on his balcony. But he hadn't turned them on since the middle of February. He didn't want to encourage winter to stay any longer. He was looking forward to sitting on his balcony watching the sailboats glide into Lake Ontario. That was some time away. Sixteen Mile Creek was still frozen.

Like most Canadians he now followed the weather forecasts with a passion. Another Colorado Low; another blast of freezing air blowing down from the Prairies. Compared to the terribly extreme cold spells in the Prairies and the never-ending snowstorms in Atlantic Canada, he knew he was lucky. He pondered about moving to British Columbia, but so much rain would remind him of miserable wet London. He accepted and loved his new surroundings, but was definitely looking forward to spring.

"How's business," Karen asked.

"I'm getting jealous of sending so many of my clients on Caribbean cruises." Ed took a sip of his beer. "I'll have to take one myself next year."

He drank his usual three beers, and paid his bill.

"Are you dropping in tomorrow night for our St. Patrick's party?"

"Do I sound Irish?" he laughed.

"You don't have to be Irish to have a good time," Karen reminded him.

He thought about it. "Sure I'll probably drop in for a beer. Just don't tell my mother when you see her next."

"We're not all bad, you know." The statement came from one of the two men standing close to him at the bar. He had a very strong Irish accent, and smiled as he spoke. He was not a regular.

"Of course you're right," Ed said, regretting his comment. "It's just that my mother sees what's going on in Northern Ireland, and the bombings in London are local and real, not just a report in the evening news."

He didn't wait for a response. He waved goodnight to Karen, stopped off at the washroom and walked to his car. He drove into the light traffic, not noticing the car that pulled out behind him. Five minutes later he entered his apartment building. The car that had followed him parked half a block away. The lights turned off. No one got out.

Ed sat looking at the phone. He was tempted to call Carolyn in Paris, but the time difference meant he would wake her at 2 a.m. Not a good idea he knew, but he did enjoy just talking to her. He'd spoken with her last weekend and had enjoyed listening to her describe her increased responsibilities. She had talked for five minutes non-stop before she apologized for carrying on like a washerwoman. She hadn't invited him to fly over to Paris, no doubt because she was so busy. He asked after her parents, both of whom he knew personally, and in the case of her father, professionally. Her father was the head of the British Secret Service, better known as MI6. Ed had worked for MI6 several times, and continued as a Consultant for them. His work was on an 'as-needed' basis—and he hadn't been needed for some months now.

What the heck he thought; he lifted the phone and started dialling her home phone number. Before he could finish, there was a loud knock on his door. He hung up the phone and walked to the door, wondering who it would be at this time of night. It was 8 p.m. He assumed it was a neighbour since no one had buzzed from the lobby.

He opened the door a few inches to have a look, but he was not quick enough to slam it closed. The door was thrown open wide and the two men from the pub pushed their way in.

"Keep your limey mouth shut," the larger man said, his Irish accent accentuated in his anger. He held a knife to Ed's stomach; close enough for Ed to feel the point of the blade against his skin.

Instinctively Ed raised his hands, not wanting to make matters worse. "What the hell . . ."

The blade was pushed further and Ed felt a trickle of blood run.

"I said shut up," the man growled, "just shut the fuck up!" His face was beet red with anger. Ed swallowed and shut up.

The second man was tearing the apartment apart, and was now in Ed's bedroom searching through every drawer tossing aside what he wasn't looking for. He finally found what he was searching for. He walked out of the bedroom holding in the air Ed's passport. He flipped through the pages. "This is him," he laughed, "our limey-American cowboy." His accent was as strong as the larger man's.

Unsure of what was happening; Ed couldn't imagine it had anything to do with his passing comment at the pub.

"Pack a bag for him," the man with the knife directed. "And make it quick." The second man ran back into the bedroom.

The man grinned as he held the knife closer and moved his face only inches from Ed' face. "You're going on a trip courtesy of the IRA. You're going to meet an old friend. An old friend from Paris." He grinned as he watched Ed's jaw drop, knowing that it was now clear why they were here.

Try as he did to show no emotion, Ed needed to throw-up. He took a deep breath and swallowed hoping to stop the three beers from re-appearing. It didn't work. He vomited to one side, just missing the man with the knife.

Ed wiped his mouth with the back of his hand, not wanting to risk reaching for his handkerchief. His mind was not on cleaning himself up; it was on Carolyn. If they had found him, they must surely have found her. Her safe location in Paris was now a sham. His head was spinning with fear. He barely heard the two men laughing at him. The second man gave him a towel and he used the time while wiping his face and hands to try and sort out the situation. The only thing he could be sure of was that he was in grave danger and he had to assume Carolyn was also. Ignorance was his only opportunity, and not a very good one at that.

"What are you talking about," he mumbled, throwing the towel on the mess on the floor.

"Don't be stupid, just do as we say." It was the second man, now standing behind him. "Take off your belt," he shouted, "now!'

Ed took of his belt and replaced it with a belt he was given from behind. He fit it tightly as he was told to do.

The man in front of him stepped back, reached into his pocked and withdrew a small plastic cigarette lighter. He flicked the lid back and held it out for Ed to see. He spoke slowly and clearly. "This is a detonator. The belt is the bomb. Do as we say and you'll live—at least a little longer. If I detonate the bomb, and be assured I will if I have to, you and everybody within six feet of you will die. Get it?"

Ed nodded. He knew what was in the belt; Semtex. The explosive the Libyan military had been selling to the IRA for years. The same explosive whose sale was being negotiated between the Libyan representatives and the IRA's Patrick Magee when he and Carolyn had managed to capture the sale on tape and camera. Their successful day in Paris was now coming back to bite them. He knew he was now in the hands of the world's most dangerous terrorists. But what of Carolyn? He couldn't get his mind off Carolyn. He would have vomited again but he had nothing left to bring up.

"I understand what you're saying," Ed said, "but I don't know what I've got to do with what you're talking about."

"Sure you don't," the first man sneered. "We'll see if the boss remembers you when we get to Boston."

"Why Boston?" Ed asked, knowing full well that thousands, if not millions, of dollars were collected in the Boston area to fund IRA activities.

"Just shut up and listen," the first man said. "My name is Tony and my friend here is Joe. Do you understand that?"

Ed nodded.

"Well we're taking a nice trip to Toronto airport and we're catching the ten o'clock flight to Boston. Do you understand that?" He didn't wait for a response. "And if you give us any agro, I blow you to smithereens. We've killed before, and we'll kill again. Do you understand that?"

Ed nodded again, trying desperately to come up with some form of action to leave a message that he had been kidnapped. He came up with nothing.

"I said do you understand that, Ed, my new friend?" He grinned at using his name.

"Yes, I do Tony," Ed took a deep breath to relax.

"Good. Then let's go," Tony said, pushing Ed toward the door. "Joe, grab his bag and keep his passport in the bag until we get to the airport." He turned to Ed. "And as a piece of insurance, mister tough guy, we have your boss nice and comfy in her office being hosted by our friend. If we don't make a phone call when we arrive in Boston, she's in trouble . . . big trouble." He grinned directly in Ed's face. "Our friend looking after her is a nasty piece of work. Keep that in mind."

Ed struggled to fully understand the risks now at hand. Diane was being held in her Burlington travel agency, and he didn't think for a moment that wasn't the truth. And he had no doubt Carolyn was at risk in Paris. His heart sank. As they left the apartment his phone rang. Ed was pushed toward the elevator. His phone continued ringing in the background as they walked down the hall.

Ed sat in the back of the car with his bag. Joe drove, and Tony sat in front on the passenger side, holding the cigarette lighter in his hand. There were several times Ed could have jumped out of the car, but if the belt he was wearing was laced with Semtex he would unquestionably be killed, and he doubted he would have had the pleasure of taking his new friends with him. He settled back, knowing he had little chance of escape. He couldn't stop thinking about Diane and Carolyn. Carolyn's part in the successful operation in Paris was far greater than his. She would be a more important target than he was. He couldn't even bear to think what they would do to her if they knew her father was the head of MI6. He closed his eyes, trying not to think of the worst. He knew he had to do as he was told. At the very least that would hopefully leave Diane unharmed, but surely emotionally shaken even in the best of circumstances. His world was collapsing around him by the minute, and there was nothing he could do about it.

When they were close to Toronto International Airport, Tony handed Ed his passport and an Air Canada ticket, and spoke as if they were friends. "You haven't been to the U.S. before according to your passport?"

Ed nodded. "Correct."

"Well your ticket is a return ticket and you're scheduled to return on Tuesday. Understand?"

Ed nodded.

"You're going down to Boston to celebrate St. Patrick's Day with your friends. Joe and me are your friends. Understand?"

"Best of friends, I'm sure."

"That's the spirit," Tony laughed. Joe joined in the laughter.

"What you probably don't know is that at Toronto Airport we pass through U.S. Customs. One of the benefits of being a good neighbour. So be very careful not to try anything clever. We'll be right with you at all times. I'll go first, then you, then Joe. Get my point."

"Yes, absolutely." Ed said.

Joe laughed. "We don't want to create an international incident, do we now?"

Tony turned and grinned. "Like blowing up a U.S. Customs officer simply because you tried something silly. You with me?"

"Fully," Ed agreed.

"Good," Tony said. "Then let's have a safe uncomplicated flight."

Toronto's Pearson International Airport, named after former Prime Minister, Lester B. Pearson in 1984, was Canada's largest airport by any measure. It was twice the size of Canada's second largest airport in Vancouver, and always busy. After turning in the rental car and making their way through the new Terminal 1, they picked up their boarding passes at the Air Canada gate. The lady at the counter offered to move them from the back row, indicating there were seats closer to the front. Tony declined the offer explaining with a laugh that they liked to be close to the washroom. Ed was impressed with their organization and charm, but the tightness of the belt around his waist kept him fully aware of their deadly potential.

They breezed through security. Tony held the cigarette lighter detonator in one hand and a pack of cigarettes in the other. "Gotta break this habit soon," he laughed to the security guard as the guard ran a metal detector over him quickly. All three passed through and walked to the U.S. Custom's officer.

Tony went first and Joe pushed Ed across the yellow line to make it clear they were travelling together. In his charming Irish accent, Tony explained to the officer they were off to ring in St. Pat's day in the most Irish of American cities. The officer almost smiled, but didn't. He stamped Tony's passport and waved Ed forward.

The officer flipped through Ed's passport, looked at the photo and then up at Ed. "Quite a world traveller," he commented. "When are you returning to Canada?"

The temptation to give a potentially confusing answer ran through Ed's head, but nothing worked. "Tuesday, sir."

The officer stamped his passport and handed it back. "Have a good trip."

An opportunity lost, Ed realized. Without clearly understanding his own thought process, he came to the conclusion that the next opportunity for action would have to be in Boston. His 'friends' would be more relaxed, being so much closer to their goal. He put any thought of escape in the back of his head. As much as he didn't want to, he again began to worry about Diane and Carolyn. He convinced himself that Diane was not at a great risk. One phone call would, if his friends were telling the truth, have her released. That was not the case for Carolyn. Where was she? Had they kidnapped her? Her parents would be worried sick. Her mother! He didn't, couldn't, bear the thought of what she would be going through. She put on a good face, but she was a mother; a mother very concerned about the career both her husband and daughter had chosen. Ed shook his head to clear his mind.

After the usual messages the ground crew started loading the plane. The first class passengers and families were boarded then the three proceeded on board to the last row of seats. Tony sat by the window, Joe was on the aisle, and Ed sat between them.

The take-off was uneventful and after they reached the plane's flying level what limited food and drink was offered was quickly and cheerfully declined by Tony for all of them. Ed sat back wishing he had been quick enough to ask for a coffee, but Tony was running the show and doing a good job.

Closing his eyes, Ed tried to envision how fast he could remove the belt. It was on the fifth or sixth hole, he couldn't remember how many. It would not be easy, of that he was sure.

Unexpectedly the safety-belt light went on, and immediately the co-pilot announced they were moving into turbulence and for all passengers to return to their seats and buckle-up. For several minutes the plane flew smoothly, then without warning Ed was shaken back to reality. There was a loud bang that was heard throughout the plane, the entire plane shook for a couple of seconds and then headed into a nosedive. People screamed while others gasped in fear. Tony and Joe looked at each other, both obviously nervous. Ed shut his eyes, not wanting to look at either of them.

"Jesus fucking, Christ," Joe gasped in fear. "I'll need a bleeding drink if we get through this."

After what seemed like an hour, but was less than a minute the plane levelled off tilting to the right. The speaker system clicked on, immediately getting everyone's attention.

"Ladies and gentlemen, this is the Captain speaking." His voice was calm; almost soothing. "I apologize for that. I'm afraid we've lost one of our engines."

"Oh, God!" a lady groaned two rows ahead of them.

The Captain continued. "This happens from time to time, and I do regret the problem. The plane is more than capable of flying on three engines, two in fact. We will, however, need to return to Toronto, disembark and put you on a new plane to complete your journey."

Sighs of relief were everywhere, including Ed and his new friends.

"In the meantime ladies and gentlemen," the Captain continued, "we need to fly at the slight angle we are now at, and I would ask that you not leave your seats. We will be on the ground in half an hour. Another plane will be ready when we get there and I'm sure you will be back on your way to Boston in less than an hour."

Few people spoke as the plane banked to turn and headed back to Toronto.

"This changes nothing," Tony said, gritting his teeth, looking at Joe. "And you'll not have a fucking drink until we get our friend here home. Understand?"

Joe nodded, angry that he had been put in his place.

Tony leaned over, smiling. "But when we do, it'll be doubles. My treat." Joe relaxed and smiled at the thought.

As the plane started its descent into Toronto, the captain came back on the speaker system.

"Ladies and gentlemen we will be landing on an emergency basis in Toronto. This is a requirement under federal aviation law, so please do not be concerned when you see emergency vehicles drive along side of us as we land. You may rest assured this will be my finest landing." There were general mummers of comfort from the passengers.

"Additionally, ladies and gentlemen, it is required that we disembark on the tarmac in a very organized and careful manner. We will leave via the front door and I would ask that you not stand up or unbuckle your safety belts until requested by one of our flight attendants."

"Shit," Tony moaned. "This is going to take forever."

It was a very smooth landing with the plane levelling off only twenty feet from touching down. The passengers applauded and many cheered. Fear was now replaced by a feeling of safety and comfort. Even seeing the emergency vehicles driving on the tarmac with their red and blue lights flashing was comforting.

It was a slow process, and Ed needed a washroom break. He wondered to himself if anyone had wet themselves. His grin got a blank look from Tony.

Two female attendants, different than the in-flight crew, were now directing the passengers off the plane. Ed heard them comforting the passengers, ensuring that everything was just fine. Something clicked in his head. He recognized a voice. He closed his eyes, put his head down, and listened. Yes, he was now sure. It was Pat's voice, he was sure . . . almost sure. He kept his head down, not wanting to look up. The two attendants were helping out the lady two rows ahead. After her, there was only the three of them left.

As the flight attendants reached them, Ed looked up. It was Pat. He didn't recognize the other attendant who was noticeably taller than Pat. For a moment, without understanding why, he wondered to himself if women as short as Pat were permitted to be flight attendants. He kept his eyes on Pat, maintaining as serious a look as he could. He felt comforted, but the semtex loaded belt was still around his waist and he couldn't safely say anything as a warning.

"Good evening, gentlemen," Pat said with a smile, "your turn now."

They each reached for their safety belts, looking down for a second as they did. It was all the time needed. Ed looked up. Pat was leaning over from the seat in front holding a gun at Tony's head, only inches away. Another gun, held by the other attendant, was in Joe's face.

"Don't move. Don't even blink." The second attendant shouted.

"What the fuck," Tony screamed. He reached into his pocket and pulled out the detonator. He held it away from everyone, with the cover flipped open. "Now you just back off from here, or I'll blow the . . ."

The sentence was never finished. There was a ear-piercing gunshot that was followed by an eerie silence. Ed had shut his eyes tight at Tony's threat. He now felt something running down his face, and when he opened his eyes he knew it was Tony's blood. Pat had pulled the trigger. She turned the gun toward Joe.

"You're next if you don't do as we say. Get it?" It was Pat's voice loud and clear, but not the Pat that Ed knew. She was staring Joe down, almost challenging him to make a move. He didn't. He looked at Pat, spat at her, and through his gritted teeth grunted. "Bitch! You're a fucking bitch."

Ed turned to Tony. The bullet had entered the centre of his forehead. What blood there was ran down his face around his lips and dripped onto his clothes. The detonator was still in his open hand. Ed looked away, wanting to wipe the blood from his own face, but somehow knew better than to make any movement.

Pat lowered the gun and held it inches from Joe's crotch. She spoke calmly. "Now do as we say, or I'll blow your balls into the middle of next week." She raised her eyebrows. "You follow?"

Joe nodded, his eyes flitting to the detonator and then to Pat. She shook her head. "I wouldn't do that if I were you. As I recall you have a lady and two little kiddies."

Joe sank into the seat, accepting the facts.

The second attendant reached into her pocket, pulled out a cloth and quickly covered Joe's face with the cloth. His eyes were wide open in fear and loathing. He refused to breath. Pat shoved her gun firmly into his crotch. Joe gasped a deep breath, tried fighting the chloroform for fifteen seconds and then collapsed.

Pat took the gun away. She closed her eyes to get a hold of what had happened. "Ed, give me the detonator," she said, her voice now shaky.

Ed reached over and gave her the detonator.

"Ed, where's the bomb?"

He gulped. "My belt. It's in my bloody belt!"

Pat grimaced. "Take it off, Ed."

He unbuckled, stepped around Joe and undid the belt. He held it out wanting to get rid of it.

"Thank you, sir," the second attendant said. "I'll look after that."

"Ed, she's RCMP. Sergeant Leah Murphy."

"Sergeant," Ed managed to acknowledge her.

She nodded in response and looked back at Joe. "He'll be out for half an hour," she said to Pat, holding up the belt. "I'll get rid of this." She walked toward the front of the plane.

Ed shook his head, now understanding the full situation. "Pat, we have a problem, a huge problem!" He was almost shouting.

Pat put a finger to her mouth. "She's safe, Ed. Carolyn's fine. I spoke to her half an hour ago. Go home. Leave the rest to . . ."

"Pat, it's not Carolyn—thank God. It's Diane. Diane Cooke, my boss. She's being held hostage in our office in Burlington." He took a deep breath. "Oh, God. If the person holding her doesn't get a phone call from these guys after landing in Boston, she's . . . I don't know what she is, but Jesus Christ we're running out of time."

Pat held up her hand to stop Ed from speaking, and shouted toward the front of the plane. "Sergeant, back here—now!"

Murphy was back in ten seconds, "Ma'am?" she asked, standing to attention.

Pat spoke as calmly as she could muster. "Leah, we have a hostage taking in Burlington. I'm taking the limo with Tyson and McDowell with me to the location. On the way we'll connect with the Halton Police. I want you to take over everything at this end." She handed her the detonator.

"Yes, ma'am."

Pat pushed Ed forward to leave the plane. "I'll be in touch later," she said over her shoulder to Murphy who was already on her cell phone, calling in extra help.

Ed and Pat ran down the passenger boarding stairs directly onto the tarmac. There were cars, ambulances, and fire engine trucks surrounding the plane, each with its different set of lights flashing, lighting up the entire area in an almost psychedelic fashion. Pat pointed to a limo set back in the fleet of cars sitting on the tarmac. They ran to the limo jumping quickly in the back seat. Pat slid open the window to the front seat where Sergeants Tyson and McDowell sat. Aware that something was an emergency, the car was moving at great speed toward the airport exit before Pat could say a word.

"Mainway in Burlington," Pat said quickly, "and patch us through to the Halton Police. I'll explain on the way." She turned to Ed. "You okay?"

Ed nodded. "Fine, thanks."

Pat gave him a faint smile. "Lower the arm rest and you'll find a pen and some paper. Drawer a diagram of the entire office, and don't leave anything out. Windows, washrooms, kitchen area, the works. Be sure to describe each entrance door. That's most important." She turned back to the sliding window. "Here's what we know, gentlemen."

Ed grabbed the pen and paper and drew the outline of the entire office building. He then filled in the meeting room, the separate offices, the washroom, the storage area, and the kitchen. He added desks and office machines to get as complete a picture as he could. He spent extra time on the doors. There was one door at the front that led into a short hallway to a second door into the office area. The rear had only an emergency exit door, solid metal. When he was satisfied with the diagram, he made notes below the drawing:

End unit—one story
Six-foot windows on two sides
Front doors all glass—both can be locked from the inside
Rear door emergency exit only—push bar
Parking lot to right-facing front. Few cars after seven pm

He reviewed the details, satisfied it was complete. He looked up at Pat who was now speaking to the officers up front. McDowell was driving, and for the first time Ed realized they were now flashing blue lights on the limo roof. The limo was speeding west on the 401. Most vehicles pulled out of their way in plenty of time. Those that didn't were driven around at breakneck speed. McDowell made no comments, he simply drove intently . . . and fast.

Tyson was on the two-way radio, co-ordinating the conversation between Pat and the Halton police. She turned to Ed. "Can we meet in the parking lot?"

"No. Way too open."

"Where?"

Ed closed his eyes to think. "Gas station on the north side of Mainway, half a block to the west."

Tyson relayed the destination and nodded to Pat as he received confirmation.

Pat turned away from the sliding window and sat facing Ed. "We're spectators on this one," she said, relaxing in the comfort of the leather seats. "But they'll wait for us to get there. They want to see your drawing for sure."

"I think you've had an exciting enough day as it is. Are you okay?"

She put her hands on her lap and exhaled, wanting her body to relax. "Yeah, yeah, I think so." She gave him a wink, but he could see the exhaustion in her face, and her hands were shaking slightly.

He reached over and took her hands in his. "Thanks for saving my life, Pat. I owe you one."

She squeezed his hands. "What are friends for, eh?"

Their conversation was brought to a halt as the limo pulled up in front of the gas station rendezvous. The four of them walked into the station retail area, through large flakes of snow softly drifting down onto the cold cement. Ed looked up to the sky. It looked like they were in for a bit of a late winter storm.

The inside of the gas station was a bee-hive of activity. Three EMS Medics were waiting patiently in the background. Ten Halton police officers, four dressed in what was generally referred to as SWAT— Special Weapons And Tactics. They were ready for action. Three of the SWAT team were men and one a woman. All four were tall, dressed entirely in black, with many pieces of equipment attached to their uniforms. They were the only officers with no name tags. The officer in charge introduced himself as Superintendent Don Craig. Although six feet tall himself, Ed was short by what was obviously the police standard in Halton. He was more than happy to be 'short'.

Pat assumed overall responsibility for the non-local authorities and handed Superintendent Craig Ed's drawing and comments. He reviewed it with the SWAT team in some detail with Ed expanding on any details they were unsure of. Other officers carefully moved outside and trained their binoculars on the building, now disappearing from sight with the snow flakes falling heavily.

Craig turned to Pat and Ed. "Do you know how many people are in there, other than Diane Cooke?"

Ed replied carefully, making it clear he was not speaking with any certainty. "The guys that took me said it was a friend. They spoke only in the singular. But . . ."

"That's fine," Craig said. "Now we know we can't make it through the front doors quickly enough; too risky. Plan A is to go through the glass on the west side of the building, directly into the middle office. We know the glass will shatter into a thousand pieces and be of no real danger. That form of glass is required by regulation. It will delay us by only two seconds. Comments?"

Pat turned to Ed. "Think it through carefully. What do you see?"

Ed closed his eyes tight to see the action in his mind and opened them with a start. "I see a problem!"

"Shit," Pat spat out. "Shit, shit, shit."

Superintendent Craig spoke calmly. "What do you see, sir?"

"The blinds," Ed replied. "There are blinds from the top of the window to the floor, and they're attached at the floor. Your team will make it through but it'll be bloody messy." He stopped to think. "Sorry, I didn't mean 'bloody' literally."

"My mother's English," he responded. "I knew what you meant."

Pat was now visibly agitated. "Superintendent, we have a time problem here. The original flight was to have landed twenty minutes ago. The guy in there is expecting a phone call as we speak. We don't know what he'll do . . ."

"We move to Plan B," Craig replied.

"Which is?" Pat asked.

"Which is you, miss. Our female officer is too tall for this to work. Here's the plan."

Ed listened in awe as the plan was outlined. It took only two minutes to outline. It was simple, quick, and dangerous: dangerous for Pat.

"Let me do it," Ed asked, clearly worried about Pat's capabilities given the day she'd experienced so far.

Pat turned to him. "Ed, you're many things, but a lady you ain't! And you're too dammed tall to boot." She walked to the washroom, undoing the buttons on her Air Canada uniform.

Superintendent Craig followed the gas station attendant to the back of the building to find the equipment Pat would need.

Ed turned to McDowell and Tyson for help. "She's ex-RCMP you know," Tyson said. "Undercover."

"She's also our ex-boss," McDowell added. "Pretty tough cookie is our Pat."

Learn something every day, Ed thought. He wanted to tell them that she had shot and killed a man earlier today, but decided against it. He knew that she could look after herself, and time was all important. While they all waited, the three male members of the SWAT team left the premises, entered an unmarked car on the north side of the parking area and drove slowly into the now heavier snow storm and quickly out of sight.

Superintendent Craig returned with a mop and a metal floor pail. He turned to Ed. "Your jacket please, and your shoes to this officer," he pointed to the female SWAT officer. "Officer," he continued, "please take this jacket and your boots to Miss Weston. If you have any make-up on you, please 'age' Miss Weston somewhat."

She removed her boots and left with a smile.

Two minutes later Pat emerged as a not-well-dressed cleaning lady. Her face was lined around her eyes and mouth. Her lipstick had been removed. Ed's jacket was too big for her, but she had somehow filled herself out to make it look acceptable. She had turned the sleeve's up inside. The jacket was down to her knees almost, which hid the Air Canada uniform. But the boots, Ed could see, did the trick. They made it look like she was waking on toffee-apples.

"How do I look?" Pat asked.

Ed jumped in first. "Like a DP just got off the ship, and I don't mean Delayed Pioneer."

"Superintendent?" she asked, waving off Ed's comments.

"Fine," he replied. "Keys to the office?" he asked Ed.

"In my jacket pocket: right side."

Pat checked for the keys picked up the mop and pail and headed to the door. "Gotta go work!" she muttered in some east European accent. "Welcome to Canada, eh!"

Superintendent Craig shook his head and looked to the sky for help. "Good luck, miss. The team is in place. They won't disappoint you. Just remember they're quick on their feet, but they're not ballet dancers."

Ed came running out of the kitchen area. "Pat, Pat, you'll need this, it's snowing." He folded a tea towel into a triangle, placed it on her head and tied it up gently under her chin. She gave him a dirty look, but left it on. She knew it was the crowning touch, but wasn't about to say so and allow him the fun of a play on words. He kissed her quickly on her forehead. "I'll be right behind you, kid. Give 'em hell."

Pat walked out into the falling snow, put her equipment into the back seat of an unmarked car, cleaned off the snow, got in and drove away.

Ed had made a promise that he intended to keep. All he needed now was a pair of shoes.

"Jesus Christ all mighty," he swore, walking from office to office, keeping his eyes on the phones at all times. "Where the fuck's that phone call? What the hell are they playing at?"

Diane moaned through the knotted rag tied around her face and mouth. She motioned with her head to the windows.

"I know it's fucking-well snowing," he shouted, "but this is Toronto, not Boston." He felt for the knife in his pocket, keeping his eyes on the phones. "Ring for Christ's sake. Ring will ya!" It didn't ring, but now his attention was immediately focused on the front door where headlights of a car shone through. He reached for the knife in his pocket.

Pat parked the car and counted to forty-five. She wanted to be seen, no surprises were needed. Turning off the car lights, Pat slowly got out of the car, and keeping her back slightly bent she collected the mop and pail and carefully walked to the front door of the travel agency. Slowly she took the keys from Ed's jacket and opened the outside door.

"Go away, go away," he screamed from behind the second door, waving his hands to get her attention. "Go away. You're too early. Go away!"

Pat put her free hand to her ear, shaking her head. "Clean office, I clean office." She spoke calmly looking at the man, holding up the mop to make her message clear. She got a good look at him through the glass doors. He was in his twenties with a slim build about five-six. Just the right height Pat thought. His hair was short; that would help.

"No! No!" he shouted louder now. "Go away!"

Pat kept waving the mop. "Clean office. Clean office."

He was now clearly exasperated by this little old woman. *Take it slowly,* he told himself, *just get rid of her.* He unlocked the second door and took the three steps to the outside door. "Look, go away and come back later." He spoke firmly, trying for an easy out.

Pat waved the mop and pail. "I leave, yes? I come back later, no?"

He raided his hands in despair, "Yeah, yeah, okay." He pushed the door open and Pat stepped inside. As she turned to leave the phone in the office rang. He quickly waved her away, turned and headed into the office through the second door.

He never made it. Pat swung the metal pail smashing him squarely on the back of his head. He screamed in pain but managed to turn toward Pat, now with a knife in his hand. He took one step toward her. She stepped back to measure her distance and thrust the mop handle into his groin with all the strength she could muster. His eyes almost popped out of his head as he slowly slid to the ground. She stepped forward, away from the outside door and stood to one side.

Instantly the SWAT team entered the agency. The first to enter was one of the men followed by the female officer. They went straight through to the main office, guns drawn. The third officer handcuffed the unconscious man's hands behind his back, and feeling certain he wasn't a risk, moved into the office area with the fourth officer behind him. It was all done silently and very quickly. Pat waited until she was waved in by the officers. She entered the main office area deliberately stepping on the man but fighting back the temptation to stomp on him with her borrowed boots.

The female officer pointed Pat into the meeting room. Diane was tied to one of the chairs, shaking in desperation and anger. Pat held up a hand. "Diane, I'm Pat from Ottawa. Ed's associate. We've spoken on the phone. Please relax. I know you don't want this, but we need some photos. We want him to go to jail, and this will help. Honest." Diane took a deep breath and relaxed.

Superintendent Craig entered, took three photos and turned to leave. "Good timing on the phone call," Pat said. Craig nodded his agreement and left.

The female SWAT officer untied Diane and removed the gag from her mouth. She left Pat and Diane to themselves.

"Did he touch you?" Pat asked. "I mean . . ."

Diane shook her head. "No," she said standing. "But I do have to go clean up." She walked carefully into the washroom area, maintaining as much poise as she could.

Ten minutes later Ed entered the meeting room. Pat and Diane were drinking a freshly brewed cup of coffee. Ed stood in the doorway looking the worse for wear. He had a towel from the gas station washroom over his head and shoulders and a plastic bag on each foot protecting his socks. He held Pat's shoes out which she was happy to take.

Diane looked at them both. "I assume this isn't a fashion show you two have prepared for me?"

Ed licked his lips, searching for the right words. "Look, Diane . . ."

"No matter, Ed," Diane said interrupting him. "Pat has outlined as much as she can. I understand. I suppose there was always a price to pay for all the government work that I get. I just wasn't expecting this."

Pat gave Ed the boots she had now removed, having slipped on her own shoes. "Ed, please return these for your shoes and ask the guys to drive you home. I have a bit of work to do before the night's out. Sergeant Murphy and I will be around your place tomorrow morning at ten. If you have time, please have a report on this evening's events as it relates to the flight. Nothing required on this activity. We're just guests on this one." She waved off his concerns about her. "Just a nice pot of tea at ten, Ed. We'll all need a nice cuppa by then."

Ed started to leave but turned to Pat. "Shall I *mop-up* as I leave?" he asked with a cheeky grin.

"Good night, Ed," Pat responded dryly.

Ed moved to leave then turned again. "Understand you had a bit of a *cock-up* with the bad guy, Pat?"

"Good night, Ed," Pat said, not looking up.

"See you Monday morning," Diane called after him.

Ed left for home.

Diane looked at Pat. "You two . . ?"

"We hug once in a while," Pat replied, raising her eyebrows. "Could do worse, I guess."

"You could do a hell of a lot worse," Diane added.

The ride home was eerily silent with the snow absorbing what little sound there was. The snow continued to drift down, creating a Christmas-card effect throughout the entire area. It wasn't until he got to this apartment door that he remembered Pat still had his keys. With less than a cheerful attitude, he headed to the on-site manager's apartment. Before knocking on the manager's door he recalled that he was alive; Carolyn was safe; Diane was in reasonable good cheer; and Pat was . . . well Pat was Pat. He knocked on the door with enthusiasm and a smile.

CHAPTER SEVEN

SATURDAY MARCH 16TH 1985

• • • ● ● ● • •

H e had barely slept. The events of the day before kept flashing through his brain. How had things gone so wrong? How did they locate him? What had actually happened to Carolyn? He felt comforted that she was safe, and reminded himself to properly thank Pat for up-dating him on Carolyn. He was seriously worried about Pat. She had changed since he had first met her just under a year earlier. She had been noticeably more relaxed, more comfortable in her job and seemingly long-term single status. He barely knew the Pat of yesterday. Cold and controlled would be the best that could be said of her words and actions. He wondered how she would be today.

He showered and shaved. It was still only just past seven. He made some tea, and reviewed the report he had written the night before. It was complete. Re-reading it made him feel better about everything that had happened. One bad man dead, all the good guys safe—at least for now. He felt better. The newspaper had no report on the incident; neither did the CBC television early-morning news. It had to be reported eventually. The media would be all over it. He turned off the TV, put on some classical music, and nodded off listening to Madame Butterfly.

The intercom woke him up. It was ten past ten. He buzzed them in and rushed to put on the kettle for tea.

They entered and Pat handed Ed his jacket and his bag recovered from the plane. She was dressed casually in blue jeans. Her eyes were puffy and her hair un-characteristically out of order.

"Sorry about the keys," Pat said rather flatly.

Leah Murphy, tall and thin, was dressed in a business suit, with no obvious signs of lack of sleep. Pat introduced her again. Ed shook her hand.

"First things first," Ed said, making the tea. He joined them in the living area. "I want to thank you both for saving my life. Whatever else is said and done about the entire matter, I want you both to understand that. I have no doubt my life wouldn't have been worth a pinch of . . . well you know what, once I was in Boston. So thank you."

Leah smiled. "Bit of a co-incidence then eh?"

Ed scrambled to understand, but couldn't. "Sorry?"

"We're having a non-Boston tea party. Things haven't come too far have they?"

Ed chuckled aloud and Pat rolled her eyes. He went to the kitchen and poured the tea. "That's funny," he said. "That is very funny."

As they drank their tea, Ed held out his report. Leah took the report and started reading it. Pat looked at Ed and gave a flat smile.

"You look pretty awful today, Ed." Pat said.

Ed smiled. "Want to borrow a mirror?"

Pat acknowledged the comment. "Yeah, I hear you."

Leah handed the report to Pat. She began to read it, her eyes widening on page one. "You puked?"

"I think the report indicates I vomited."

"Whatever." She read it with some speed, and turned to Ed. "What do you mean, and I quote, 'I assumed the flight attendant pulled the trigger'. Do you think he committed suicide for Christ's sake?"

Leah interrupted Ed's response. "I take it you mean you did not see the gun actually go off, and the man may have reached up to grab the gun away from the flight attendant's hand?"

"My report is what it is," Ed replied. "I assumed what I assumed."

"That's bull," Pat said angrily.

Leah turned the report to page three. "I have just one question on your very complete report, if I may?"

Ed waved her on, knowing what was coming.

"You state that the men convinced you they would kill you since they mentioned their involvement in the Newry attack? I assume you know they would have been referring to the deaths of nine police officers in Newry in Northern Ireland just last month?"

"Absolutely," Ed said.

Pat raised her hand, and looked him coldly in the eyes. "Is that absolutely-that is what they said, or absolutely-that is what they were referring to?"

"Absolutely both," he lied.

Pat finished her tea, keeping her eyes on him over the cup.

"One more question, Ed," Leah said, noticing the vibes between them, "and this is important. Did either of the men leave you at any time from the moment they entered your apartment?"

Pat made the point. "And this is important, Ed!"

Ed shook his head. "They were not out of my sight for a second during the entire process. And before you ask, Pat, we went to the washroom together. Three stalls in a row."

"Charming I'm sure," Pat retorted. "Three birds on a wire. A Crowe and two vultures."

Leah stood, gave Pat the report, and walked to the door. "That does it for me. Pat has some information I'm not cleared to hear. Job well done and a damn good report." She looked at Pat as she spoke. Ed escorted her to the door.

"I was hoping you'd be in uniform," Ed smiled, "you'd look good in red."

"Next time, perhaps," Leah responded. She closed the door quietly as she left.

Pat shook her head in disgust. "Jesus Christ, Ed. You're flirting with an RCMP officer, in front of me no less."

"Not flirting, Pat, just playing the role of a gentleman."

"You ain't no gentleman." She waved him off and gathered herself. "Actually, you are quite a gentleman. Sorry."

He bowed slightly, topped up their tea and they sat at the kitchen table.

Pat waved the report in the air. "But you're a liar, Ed, a damn liar. A damned good liar perhaps, but a liar none-the-less."

"Are you refusing to accept my report?"

She shrugged. "It's not for me to accept or reject it. I just pick it up and submit it with mine."

Ed waited to speak, changing the subject. "You look tired, Pat, are you okay?"

She looked over at him, tears now running down her face. "I killed a man, Ed. I shot him through his head. How the hell am I supposed to feel? Good? How do I tell my mother?" She shook her head and wiped away her tears. "But I can't tell her, can I? I can tell her I've got a lover, but I can't tell her I killed a man. What kind of a life is that? Oh shitting hell!" She dropped her head, trying to hide her tears and embarrassment.

He chewed on his lips, thinking carefully. "Can I ask you a couple of questions?"

"No you damn well cannot. Please don't patronize me."

"Is that a play on words? *Pat*ronize?"

"Oh give over, Ed." She lifted her head and wiped her eyes dry. He reached for a Kleenex and she blew her nose. She sat up straight in the chair re-capturing her composure. "What questions, Ed?"

"Did the belt contain explosives?"

She sniffed, "Yes, Semtex."

"Was the detonator activated to set it off?"

"Yes."

"How much damage could it have done?"

She raised her hands in uncertainty. "Half of the plane would have been destroyed. We're not exactly sure."

"So it seems to me . . ." he started, but she interrupted.

"Don't you start playing your word games with me, Ed. The man's dead. I killed him."

He raised his eyebrows and shrugged.

"Okay, Ed," she gave in, "what does it *seem* to you?"

He took her hand in his. "Pat, I was with those blokes, . . ."

"Guys."

"I was with those guys, Pat. He *would* have pressed the trigger. He'd be dead, I'd be dead, the other guy would be dead, and both you and Leah would be dead." He squeezed her hand. "Look I'm not saying you shouldn't be concerned that he's dead, but you've got to totally understand that the alternative was five dead—him plus four more." He grinned slightly. "And hey, one of those would have been your lover; as in me." He looked at her seriously. "Pat, you saved my life. I know that for sure. And yes, you won't be able to tell your mother that you killed a man, but neither will I be able to tell my mother that you saved my life."

She thought about his words. "That's doesn't compute. It's hardly the same thing is it?"

He grimaced. "Not really, no. But to my mother it would be. If I could tell her that is, which I can't."

She pushed his hand away. "You're trying to confuse me, and not doing a bad job at that."

"That's double negative Pat."

"Shut up, Ed. Okay, I'm feeling a little better. Get us some more tea and I'll bring you up-to-date on what happened."

He took their cups to top them up.

"Ed," she said, talking to his back.

"Yes, Pat?"

"Thanks for that. I mean it. You're an okay bloke."

He nodded acknowledgement and filled the kettle.

He carried over two fresh hot cups of tea. Pat had wiped away the tears. She looked more relaxed and smiled as she lifted the cup with both hands to sip her tea.

"England's answer to the problems of the world?" she asked, holding her cup out.

"You'd think so watching Coronation Street, wouldn't you?" Ed agreed, nodding. "There's some truth to it I suppose. Few people have booze in their house. That's what the pubs are for, right?"

"Speaking of," Pat said. "I phoned the Queen's Head last night about twenty minutes after you had left. I then phoned you at home for about half an hour. When you didn't answer, then I knew there was a problem."

Ed thought for a moment. "Didn't think I would have a date then?"

"It crossed my mind actually. But I really didn't think you'd go to the pub, and then go out. You'd take your date there first." Pat smiled. "Been there, done that. Right?"

"You've got me there," he laughed. "The phone did ring just as we, that's my new friends and myself, were leaving for the airport and then onto Boston."

Pat took a long drink of her tea, and put the cup down. "Let me start from the beginning. Last night's activities didn't eliminate the problems; I'd guess we may have made them worse."

Ed pulled a face.

"Anyway," Pat continued, "back to the beginning. There was a very unfortunate leak from the British Embassy in Paris last Christmas. Unintended and unfortunate, but a serious leak never-the-less. A staff member of the Embassy who was aware of the IRA meeting with the Libyan representatives, and of course Carolyn's and your involvement in it, let the details slip. More booze related than stupidity, but who cares?"

"Do I know the person?"

"Yes."

"Shit. Terry. The receptionist!"

Pat nodded. "Luckily, and thank God, she realized her mistake and confessed fully. Letter of resignation, the works. The result was a doubling of the surveillance activities on both the IRA and Libya. What London saw were four active members of the IRA leave Dublin, two for Paris and two for Boston. The Paris trip was an obvious message. Carolyn was put under constant cover, and the two men were arrested by the Paris police for breaking and entry, or whatever they call it in France. They were caught hiding in Carolyn's apartment. No reference is being made to their IRA activities. We want to separate the crimes. Proving they were there as IRA participants with intent to kidnap, or whatever, simply wouldn't hold. So they went for the lesser crime, and those two are going to prison. That's a slam-dunk." She rapped the table with her knuckles.

"And the Boston duo?"

"Well, that took a little longer. IRA members going to Boston is hardly a rare occasion, especially around St. Patrick's Day. It was only the nagging in the back of Carolyn's head that had her get in touch with one of her contacts in Washington. Washington's quick action identified that the Boston duo were now heading back to Boston after a quick trip to Toronto about the same time that I was notified by US Customs you were boarding the same plane. It worked wonderfully. Those US guys can be a pain sometimes, but they know how to do their job."

"Thank God."

"In God we trust, and all that," Pat mused. "Anyway, the plan was simple. Let the plane take off; arrange for an engine to fail, and have it fly back to Toronto on emergency procedures. The emergency vehicles allowed all kinds of attendees; RCMP, local Police, airport Police, even OPP. We were loaded for bear."

"That's good to know."

"I flew down from Ottawa in this amazing jet, and the rest is history."

"Why you?"

"We wanted you to recognize my voice. I hope you did. I felt like I was shouting at times."

"I recognized you," Ed said proudly, "and felt safer immediately."

"Yeah, sure ya did. You looked scared stiff to me."

"Had to play the role, right?"

"Good acting then."

"So I owe both you and Carolyn a big thank you."

"You sure do."

Pat took their cups and refilled them.

"So now what?" Ed asked.

"We're not sure, and even if we were I'm not sure I would tell you. But going back to Leah's question, Ed, it is important that neither man left you at any time. That is hugely important." She looked at him seriously.

"Pat, I promise you, neither one left my sight." He took a deep breath. "Can I take it that since they did not, then they obviously had no time to contact anyone, and you can work out a strategy that is based on my kidnapping never happening?"

"Very good, Ed. Exactly. So officially it never happened."

"Does Carolyn head back to Paris?"

"Tomorrow."

"Like nothing happened."

"Absolutely."

"And what about Terry?"

"Like nothing happened, right? She's back in her role as receptionist, deeply embarrassed, having learned a very expensive lesson. Her father, who as you may know is an MP, flew to Paris and read the riot act in no uncertain terms." She shrugged. "So it's business as usual. Speaking of which, I'd like you to go to The Queen's Head tonight for a St. Paddie's drink. Okay?"

Ed shrugged. "If you insist!"

"Yeah, right. For queen and country I'm sure. Anyway, that's all we know on the first part of yesterday's fun and games."

"How's Diane?" Ed asked, feeling guilty he hadn't asked earlier.

"She's fine. Spoke to her this morning—in the office, no less. She works hard."

"That time of year," Ed said. "I'll pop in to see her later. What do we know about the guy?"

"A local bad guy; Jack DiCosimo. Out of Hamilton actually. Works at Stelco, when he works that is."

"Not Irish?"

"Does his name sound Irish?" Pat laughed.

"I guess not."

"You're right on the ball sometimes, Ed. No, he was just hired to do the job. Hold Diane until the phone call came in and then take off."

"What about Diane?" Ed asked quickly. "He couldn't just . . ."

Pat interrupted. "He could, and he would, but there's a catch. And the catch tells us how organized all this was." She paused. "Well, whaddya think the catch was?"

Ed stopped to think but nothing clicked. "Sorry, my brain's having a slow-down."

Pat nodded. "I understand; you're male." She was enjoying this. "Guess who showed up at 1a.m., just as we were *cleaning* up?"

"Of course," Ed said, tapping his head, "the regular cleaning lady!"

"Exactly. So Diane would have been freed all right, but only after a long cruel wait."

"Clever bastards, those IRA blokes." He nodded at Pat. "So was the regular cleaner old and haggard-looking as ours was last night?" He waited for a rude response, but didn't get one.

"No, actually she's a twenty-two year old university student working her way through four years of Commerce."

"Oh, really?" Ed mused. "Maybe I should work late on Fridays?"

Pat shook her head. "No, she's not your type. She's tall, slim, very good looking, and super intelligent."

"And you're point is? I like super intelligent young ladies."

"Good answer, Ed. You just dodged a bullet." Realizing what she had said, she held up her hands in despair. "Listen to me. I can't even think straight before I speak."

Ed changed the subject. "What's the story on our Mr. DiCosimo?"

"Oh yeah, him. He's agreed to plead guilty to break and entry, no reference to Diane."

Ed shook his head. "What?"

"Think about it. He goes to jail for five years, less than the maximum with his history, and agrees to say nothing about the hostage taking."

"And?"

"And the IRA people that hired him, and they were IRA, will think he was arrested before he had a chance to hold Diane."

"It won't work surely?"

"It'll work fine . . . Diane was out for a client meeting. When she returned she saw him in the office, phoned the police and as you say, Bob's your uncle. And I have to go."

"Why don't you lie down for a while, you look like you haven't slept for a week."

"There you go," she said, walking to the door, "using all you charm on me again."

He caught up to her at the door. He put his arms around her and squeezed her tight. "Thanks for everything," he said, kissing her forehead.

"Thanks for the report." She opened the door. "It'll help."

"See you in June," he called after her. "Keep in touch."

She called back. "June it is. You'll get a phone call in fifteen minutes!"

Ed grabbed for the phone when it rang.

"Still alive!" he quipped.

"Glad to hear it, Mr. Crowe," Lord Stonebridge said respectfully. "Haven't lost your sense of humour then?"

Ed groaned inwardly. "I'm sorry sir, I assumed . . ."

"That's fine, Mr. Crowe; I'll put her on in just a few minutes if you can wait?"

"Yes of course, sir."

"I won't take much of your time, Mr. Crowe. I gather you're fine? These things can take a toll you know?"

"It was easier for me than others, sir, and not to put too fine a point on it—my first statement is correct."

"Yes, of course you are and I can assure you we've all been following the events over there with great interest and concern of course. The Canadian team did a superb job."

"Yes they did. Especially . . ."

"Yes, I understand." He paused to make his point. "I suppose you have documented everything?"

"Yes sir. It's in transit."

"Well done, Mr. Crowe. Perhaps when I get our copy we could chat? Would a trip over here be out of the question?"

"No, sir," he replied enthusiastically. "It would give me a chance to visit my mother."

"And others too, I'm sure."

"Yes, sir."

"Then I look forward to seeing you in a couple of weeks, Mr. Crowe. My secretary will be in touch. For now I'll pass you on to Miss Andrews. Remember this call is being recorded. I'll head downstairs and see if Lady Stonebridge is conversing with me yet."

"Hello, Ed," Carolyn said. "How is she?"

"A little better now than an hour or two ago, but she's sure shook up. She left just a few minutes ago."

"She's a strong one, but that's a big burden to carry. Let's hope she pulls through."

"I have a lot to thank you for, Carolyn."

"Just returning the favour, Ed." He knew she was referring to her own kidnapping in Sofia the previous year, and the work he had performed to help set her free.

"Well I still owe you a beer. Will you be in England when I visit in a week or so?"

"No, I'm sorry I'll be in Paris."

"Oh," was all he could muster.

She giggled. "Of course I'll be here, silly. I'm your joint sponsor aren't I?"

"You're that at the very least," he said, now grinning. "How's Lady Stonebridge?"

He heard her take a long deep breath. "Let's just say she continually wants to discuss my career aspirations."

"She is your mother," he threw in.

"Hey, whose side are you on here?"

"My side." He left it at that.

"Hmm," Carolyn replied. "Look I have to go. Listen to this," she said excitedly, "I'm going to meet my father's boss!"

Ed was impressed. Her father's boss was the Prime Minister, Mrs. Thatcher. "I am both impressed and jealous," he said. "I look forward to seeing you soon."

"Likewise, Ed," she said. They hung up.

CHAPTER EIGHT

LATER THAT DAY

• • • • • •

E d walked into the Queen's Head at five-thirty. The St. Patrick's
Day party was just warming up. The bar was decorated for the
occasion. Green was everywhere and the staff wore Guinness tee
shirts, also appropriately green. The still small crowd was in a mood
to party.

"Ed, you made it," Karen said, holding up a glass. "Double D. or the
real Irish drink?" she asked, gesturing to the Guinness tap.

"Just the usual, please. Tradition and all of that!"

"A lady phoned for you last night," Karen said, winking. "Did she
get hold of you?"

"Yes she did thanks."

"Hmm, must be nice when the ladies are tracking you down."

"She's from Ottawa."

"So did you hear the big news?" Karen asked, pulling his beer.

"Ireland ran out of beer?" Ed quipped.

"No, a couple of guys blew themselves up at one of the hotels by the
airport. One's dead, and the other one's in serious condition."

He reached for his beer and took a long hard swallow. "No, I missed
it." He spoke as casually as his nerves would let him. "What's the story?"

Karen shrugged. "Lots of mystery it seems. Apparently they were
carrying some kind of plastic explosive and something went wrong. No
names released, all they said was that they weren't Canadian."

Karen left to serve other customers. Someone turned off the television and loud Irish music filled the pub. The music seemed to work like magic. The customers got louder and some began singing. Ed looked into his beer. He worked out what he thought the details would be. One man dead, the other in some kind of a coma that needed twenty-four hour nursing. All personal information, including their passports, destroyed. The media would ask a few questions and then all eyes would be turned to the celebration of St. Patrick's Day and the bombing would be quickly forgotten. That seemed almost bizarre, he thought.

Peter, the bar manager, leaned over the bar to Ed. "Are you expecting a friend?"

Ed shook his head.

"Some Irish guy just phoned and asked if you were here. I told him you were, and then he just hung up. I thought it might be a friend looking to join you." Peter shrugged and left to go back to his thirsty customers.

Ed was tempted to look around to see if someone was watching him, but he knew better than to do so. He took a drink of his beer and enjoyed the music.

Twenty minutes later Peter stood by the end of the bar with the phone in his hand, waving to Ed that there was a phone call for him. Ed worked his way to the phone, being sure not to spill anyone's drinks as he manoeuvred carefully through the now lively crowd. He covered an ear as he spoke loudly into the phone. "Happy St. Patrick's Day, my man," he said with a smile.

"Are you drunk?" Pat asked.

"Certainly not, young lady, I'm still working on my first beer. How can I be of assistance?"

There was a slight pause. "Wanna share a pizza?" Ed could tell she was reluctant to ask.

He tried not to shout too loud. "Absolutely. One-hundred percent. Where are you?"

"At your place."

"In the lobby?"

"In your apartment," she said sheepishly.

Ed thought for a second. "I didn't know . . . It doesn't matter. I'll be there in ten. I won't even finish my beer."

Pat laughed. "Finish it. I want to clean up a bit."

A thought flashed through Ed's mind. "Okay, but don't order out. I'll make a special meal for us. Okay with you?"

"Hey, I like being spoiled, even by a bloke who can't cook." She hung up.

Ed managed to collect his beer then headed toward the kitchen area, chuckling as he thought through the special meal he had in mind.

He entered his apartment carrying a bag of goodies that he would not let Pat look into as much as she tried. He made her promise to stay out of the kitchen as he prepared his special meal. Pat sat across the room, sipping on her glass of wine.

"Hey, look," she said, wanting to get the misunderstanding out of the way, "the reason I didn't mention I had a key to this place was, well . . . sort of . . . you know?"

He shook his head. "No, I don't know, and really don't care. I'm glad you have a key and further I'm glad you felt comfortable enough to use it tonight," he gave her a wink, "or any other night for that matter."

She nodded. "Thanks." She needed to change the discussion. "You know a man called the pub looking for you, right?"

Ed looked up, amazed at her knowing that so quickly. "How did you . . ."

"We bugged the phone of course. That's why we wanted you to go to the pub. We knew they would phone or be there to see you in person. Gotta get up early . . ."

Ed stopped his preparations. "You had someone there, in the Queen's Head?"

"Yep, and don't ask. You don't know the person and likely will never meet him or her. So don't ask."

"You're scary, you know that?"

Pat grinned a mighty grin. "Yep, and thanks." She sipped her wine. "So what are you cooking?"

"A special meal for a special friend. An English gourmet meal."

Pat laughed aloud. "English gourmet cooking! That's like German humour, French manners. It's called an oxymoron—a contradiction in terms."

"You'll see," Ed replied. "This is something very special." As he spoke, he opened the oven door and slid in his special meal. "Thirty minutes and we'll be ready to eat."

He joined her on the sofa and clinked their glasses. "To English gourmet cooking," he toasted.

"To mission impossible," Pat answered.

After setting the table and pouring them another glass of wine, he invited Pat to come to the table.

"Now close your eyes for a moment while I bring out the cuisine de evening," Ed asked, looking forward to the special meal. Pat was happy to oblige and quite intrigued.

"Voila!" Ed exclaimed as he brought the glass baking pan to the table. "You can open your eyes now."

Pat opened her eyes and sat back. She looked at the dish, then at Ed and then back to Ed's special meal.

"What the hell is that?" she asked, not holding back her disgust.

"That, my dear, is toad-in-the-hole."

"What!"

"Toad-in-the-hole. An English specialty."

She shook her head. "To me it looks like a penis pie."

"Pat, please," was all he could muster. "I went to a lot of work for this."

"Well I hope you don't expect me to eat those things? They look disgusting."

"They're English bangers."

"Oh, bangers are they? More sexual innuendo."

"They're English bangers cooked in Yorkshire pudding. Remember; no sex please we're British!"

"I can't believe we're looking at a four-penis pie and not a pepperoni and mushroom pizza."

Ed cut the pie in half, giving each one of them two sausages each.

"How come I get the small penises?" Pat asked. "Is this intended to reflect the real world?"

Ed closed his eyes and his head sank to his chest. He knew he was Pat's only lover. He opened one eye to Pat. "Not nice."

Pat grinned and picked up her knife and fork. "If these things spit at me when I start on them, you're in big trouble, Mr. English Chef."

"Not a problem, they've been pricked."

"There you go again!" she said, dropping her cutlery. "In-the-hole, bangers, and now they're pricked. I ain't eating these sex objects."

"Trust me," Ed said cutting into his first banger. "You'll love them."

"If I'm going to eat these, I want a steak knife."

Ed quickly brought her a serrated steak knife, and sat to watch her. To his horror she started on the larger banger and sliced it carefully from end to end, grinning with pleasure as she did. She did the same with the second banger, obviously enjoying the surgery. She took a deep breath and smiled. "That's shows them who the boss is," she laughed. "And don't you forget it, Mr. Crowe."

They ate their meal in peace, each convinced they had won the day. Ed had forced Pat to relax. Pat had made sure she was still the boss.

It was a most enjoyable meal.

Pat gave Ed a hug as she prepared to leave to see her parents before returning to Ottawa the next day.

"See you in June then," Ed murmured.

"You did your job well this evening," Pat said standing at the door.

"Sorry?" Ed acted dumb.

Pat laughed. "You're so transparent, Edwin William. Thanks for everything. I feel one heck of a lot better than I did this morning, toad-in-the-hole and all." She closed the door quietly as she left.

I thought it tasted pretty good, he said to himself. *Maybe I could get a part-time job at The Head? All those young, good looking girls. Nahh, maybe not. Too much like hard work.*

He started cleaning up, satisfied with the results of the day.

CHAPTER NINE

FRIDAY MARCH 22ND 1985

• • • • • • •

M r. Cooper met him at London's Heathrow airport. Ed had taken the late flight from Toronto and it was now seven thirty in the morning, London time.

"Not used to getting up quite this early," Mr. Cooper said, shaking Ed's hand. "It's great to see you, Eddie. You're looking fine."

"Thanks, Mr. Cooper, you're looking pretty sprightly yourself. Semi-retirement must suit you."

Mr. Cooper nodded. "It does, Eddie. Two more months working with the new owners, and I pull the plug."

Mr. Cooper had owned and run his own travel agency since before the war. It was now the most successful agency in the Kensal Rise area of London. Ed had worked for Mr. Cooper for many years and it was Mr. Cooper's involvement in MI6 that had led to Ed's now consulting with them. He was more than a friend to Ed; he was also a father figure. Ed's father had died when Ed was two years old and his mother had raised him alone.

The limousine pulled up in front of the terminal and Mr. Cooper and Ed with his bag got in. Mr Cooper closed the sliding door to the driver. It wasn't essential to do so, since the driver was also a member of MI6.

"Force of habit," Mr. Cooper explained. "Okay, Eddie, I've read your report. Lord Stonebridge has read it of course along with the reports from CSIS and the RCMP. But tell me in detail all about your recent experience. Let me preface it with the comment that things are getting a lot more dangerous for you than I ever expected. We should discuss your on-going relationship as a consultant with Lord Stonebridge." He took a deep breath. "But for now, tell me all."

As they drove to Stonebridge Manor, along the back roads as best the driver could, it was through an expanse of spring flowers—each seeming to do their best to capture the sun's warmth. Ed reviewed the events in as much detail as he could.

Mr. Cooper pulled a face and shook his head as Ed described the actual shooting. "In all my years involved with the department, I've never had to do anything like that. How is Miss Weston? She sounds rather tough."

Ed shook his head. "Not really. She did what she had to do. I doubt she's had a good night's sleep since, and that was a week ago."

Mr. Cooper nodded his understanding. "What counts is that she did the right thing. She deserves a medal in my mind. If for no other reason than I didn't have to call on your mother to tell her you were a goner. God, I dread the thought!"

Ed recounted the remainder of the details just as they pulled up in front of Stonebridge Manor.

The maid answered the door.

"Usual process, Eddie," Mr. Cooper said. "Lady Stonebridge would like to see you. You know where. I'll see you upstairs. Take your time," he said smiling, almost grinning, knowing full well Ed was in for an interesting chat.

Ed gently rapped on the huge drawing-room door and entered. Lady Stonebridge was sitting in her usual chair, dressed for the occasion.

"Come in, Edwin. Have a seat."

"Good morning Lady . . ." but she interrupted him by raising her hand. "Good morning Mrs. S," he continued. "How are you this fine spring day?"

They had agreed on this less formal greeting when she had visited him in Canada. Neither Lord Stonebridge nor Carolyn was aware of the visit. Her goal in visiting had been to encourage Ed to make better contact with Carolyn in Paris. As it turned out, his visit to Paris had set the stage for the most recent kidnapping attempts by the IRA. A fact he knew better than to mention.

Lady Stonebridge folded her hands on her lap. "I am well, thank you. How are you, Edwin, and how is your mother?"

"We are both fine, thank you. I'm seeing her tomorrow."

"Excellent. I'd like to meet her sometime. Does she come out this way from time to time?"

Ed had to think fast. "I don't wish to sound parochial Mrs. S., but my mother would feel a tad Eliza Doolittle in these surroundings."

"That's not being parochial, Edwin," Lady Stonebridge shot back, "that's being snobbish. When you see her tomorrow, please extend an open invitation to your mother to visit us. My husband inherited the estate he didn't build it. There is a significant difference of course."

"Of course," Ed said, regretting his comment. "I will certainly relay the invitation."

"Good. That is settled. Now about my daughter." Lady Stonebridge lifted her head to make direct eye contact. "I take it you are still in love with her."

"Yes I am."

"Good. I suspect she would be disappointed to know otherwise. Is she travelling with you to see your mother?"

Ed shrugged. "I haven't had the chance to ask her as . . ." Lady Stonebridge, picking up a small bell and ringing it, interrupted him. Almost immediately the maid entered the room.

"Please ask my daughter to join us, Miriam. And if she pulls a face, please let her know I would like her to escort Mr. Crowe to Lord Stonebridge's office. I think that is where you will find her."

Miriam left the room, as quiet as a mouse.

"Lovely weather," Ed said.

"Quite lovely," Lady Stonebridge agreed. "Lovely enough for Carolyn to have arranged a picnic for the two of you."

Ed smiled at the idea.

Lady Stonebridge frowned. "I only wish she had the capability of cooking the food herself." As she spoke, Carolyn entered the room. She turned to Ed smiling and they shook hands. Carolyn nodded to her mother.

"I didn't invite you here to shake hands with Mr. Crowe," Lady Stonebridge said calmly.

Carolyn rolled her eyes, but Ed took the opportunity to kiss her cheek, holding the kiss for ten seconds.

"May I leave now, Mother?" Carolyn asked.

Lady Stonebridge didn't answer the question. "Mr. Crowe is visiting his mother tomorrow. If I may be so rude as to ask, but would you be planning to join him—assuming you were invited that is?"

Ed grinned at Carolyn.

"Nothing," Carolyn said, turning to her mother, "would make me happier. May I borrow the Jag?" She turned to Ed. "Will Roy be there?"

"Roy?" Lady Stonebridge queried.

Carolyn couldn't miss the opportunity. "Roy is Mr Crowe's best friend, Mother. A very nice person, rather wealthy, and he has asked for my hand in marriage."

Lady Stonebridge gasped, and coughed to settle herself.

"And tomorrow," Carolyn continued, "will be a perfect time to give him my answer. Don't you think so, Mr. Crowe?"

Ed only nodded, not wanting to get between the contestants.

"Marriage?" Lady Stonebridge gasped. "You?"

"Fear not, Mother," Carolyn said, enjoying the moment, "you won't have to dip into your special bank account as yet. I intend to gracefully decline Roy's most generous offer."

"I see," Lady Stonebridge managed. She re-settled herself on the sofa, the colour slowly returning to her face. "My reason for asking, before you led us in other directions, was for you to invite Mrs. Crowe to join us as a guest sometime at her convenience."

"Why, Mother," Carolyn said, now smiling pleasantly, "what a lovely thought on your part. I will be sure to do that, and I shall insist that she accepts."

"Thank you, dear." Lady Stonebridge had now resumed her leading role. "And, Mr. Crowe, please join us for dinner tonight, and I insist you stay with us overnight as our special guest."

"Thank you, Lady Stonebridge," Ed said, knowing not to call her Mrs. S., in front of Carolyn.

Lady Stonebridge maintained the upper hand. "You should both now meet with Lord Stonebridge. I have kept you long enough."

Ed and Carolyn left the room, kissed quickly, and walked swiftly up to Lord Stonebridge's office, grinning like a couple of school kids.

Lord Stonebridge walked around his desk to greet Ed. "Welcome, Mr. Crowe. I trust your meeting with Lady Stonebridge went well?" He had a slight smile.

"Very well, sir, thank you very much. She is always interested in how my mother is doing."

"In fact," Carolyn added, "Mr. Crowe has been requested to invite his mother to the manor when he visits her tomorrow. Since I will be joining him, I will make the invitation myself."

"Excellent idea," Lord Stonebridge said. "And you and your wife should join us also, General," he said turning to Mr. Cooper, calling him by his traditional MI6 name. "We'll make a weekend of it."

Mr. Cooper nodded. "The pleasure will be ours, Lord Stonebridge. I shall make the arrangements once I hear from Miss Andrews that the invitation has been made and accepted."

"Yes, I like that idea a great deal," Lord Stonebridge said, inviting them all to sit around his desk. "But for now, to business."

Ed took the chair closest to the desk, as was the custom when he was visiting on business.

"So, Mr. Crowe," Lord Stonebridge said, gently rubbing his chin, "interesting times?"

"Perhaps an understatement?" Mr. Cooper pondered aloud.

Lord Stonebridge accepted the comment with a smile. "A bad trait of mine, General, at least according to Lady Stonebridge. Point taken though. Mr. Crowe?"

"Interesting indeed, sir. And while I don't want to underestimate the significance of what happened both in Canada and in Paris, it does seem to me that the combined resources of your department, the CIA, and CSIS did a wonderful job of intercepting the kidnappers at both ends."

"Very true, and due in no small part to Miss Andrew's work at this end."

"Thank you, sir," Carolyn said, trying unsuccessfully to avoid blushing.

Ed bit his lip quickly, knowing he had to admit an error. "There is one thing, sir," he said, "before we go over my report in detail."

Lord Stonebridge waved him on.

"I think I made a mistake by saying that the two men that kidnapped me told me they were part of the Newry attack."

"Really?" Lord Stonebridge said, looking down at the papers in front of him. "Please continue."

"What they did say, was that they had killed before, and I jumped to the conclusion that they had meant Newry since it had happened only weeks before. I'm sorry, sir."

"That is interesting, Mr. Crowe," Lord Stonebridge said, flipping through the papers, "because the CSIS report suggests that you likely jumped to that conclusion. It was obviously written by a most observant person."

"That would probably be Miss Weston," Carolyn said, "the lady that fired the shot."

"Yes of course," Lord Stonebridge agreed. He turned to Ed. "Have you spoken or seen her since, Mr. Crowe?"

Ed outlined his meeting with Pat and Sergeant Murphy the morning following the shooting and the second meeting with Pat later that evening.

"A brave lady," Lord Stonebridge said. "Of course the fact that the weapons they were carrying were loaded with live ammunition makes it clear that she had the authority to shoot to kill. Do we all agree?"

Everyone agreed. But Ed was aware that the message to him was that there was no need for him to adjust his report in order to help Pat in her actions.

Lord Stonebridge made a note on his papers. "Then let's put that minor difference down to an honest and, I would add, an honourable error."

"Well put," Mr. Cooper said from behind. "Now, Eddie, why don't you go over your report minute by minute so that we all have a full understanding of the events?"

Ed recounted the events of the day of the kidnapping in as much detail as he could recall. The others listened intensely, asking questions as he recalled the actions. It was difficult for them to hear the facts of the actual shooting. The detail that Ed offered made it seem that it was happening as they listened. He didn't let the expressions on their faces slow him down. If anything it helped him continue without stopping. When he was finished, the room fell silent for a minute.

"Amazing," was all that Lord Stonebridge could muster, shaking his head. He ordered tea. The conversation turned to other matters while they waited. Shortly the tea arrived and they helped themselves.

"So tell me, Mr. Crowe," Lord Stonebridge asked, sipping his tea, "what exactly did Miss Weston say to the second man to get him to calm down?"

Ed thought back for a moment. "She pointed her gun at his, ahem, private parts and advised him if he didn't do as he was told, she would transfer his testicles into the middle of next week—sir."

"Oh my goodness," Mr. Cooper said, crossing his legs.

Lord Stonebridge carefully put down his cup of tea. "Indeed," he muttered.

"She's not one to beat about the bush," Carolyn added, trying not to smile.

"And then she reminded him he had a wife and two children," Ed said quickly.

"That was a nice touch," Lord Stonebridge said, happier now he had asked the question.

Everyone nodded in agreement.

"And then they used the chloroform on him?" Lord Stonebridge asked.

"Only after Pat encouraged him, sir," Ed said, now enjoying the telling of the details. "She thrust the barrel of the gun into his private parts. That action made him breathe in rather deeply."

Mr. Cooper pulled a face. "That doesn't sound like cricket, does it?"

"Baseball, General," Carolyn added, now smiling. "Tagged out at home plate!"

Mr. Cooper shook his head. "You really do have a way with words, Miss Andrews."

"Yes indeed," Lord Stonebridge agreed.

"Sorry, gentlemen," Carolyn said with modesty. "It's just that what she did worked."

They all nodded in agreement.

"Are you aware, Mr. Crowe," Lord Stonebridge asked, "what happened to the second man?"

Ed shook his head.

Lord Stonebridge explained. "Well the media reports correctly outlined at that time he was in a coma. While that was correct at the time, it was in fact a medically induced coma. He is now under arrest under the War Measure Act, an Act I might add, quite unique to Canada. I won't go into the details of the Act, but it's fair to say it provides very wide powers to the Canadian government in the event of certain perceived dangers."

"But there is no war." Ed queried.

"No," Lord Stonebridge agreed. "But in the need for national security for, and I quote, '. . . defence, peace, order and welfare of Canada . . .' the Act can be, and has previously been enforced. It was most recently enforced in October 1970 during what is generally referred to in Canada as 'the October Crisis'".

"And the man?" Carolyn asked.

"Is where the government wants him to be," Mr. Cooper answered.

Ed was amazed. "And the IRA?"

"Yes, the IRA," Lord Stonebridge said emphatically. "We have absolutely no doubt they are aware their man is alive and under arrest. Luckily for us, the IRA has few contacts in Canada—unlike the U.S. that is—so he is in a perfect spot for questioning."

"And of course," Mr. Cooper added with a smile, "there is no chance the IRA will negotiate to trade him. To do so they would have to admit to the entire kidnapping in the first place. No, he's worth nothing to them as a bargaining chip."

"And the good thing," Lord Stonebridge added with some pleasure, "is that he knows it."

Carolyn summed it up. "So the only bargaining to be done is between the Canadian authorities and a very lonely soldier in a foreign country, about whom no one cares much about."

"Precisely," Lord Stonebridge said.

"Tell us about the evening events," the General asked.

Ed described the events from his and Pat's leaving the plane and the kidnapping and ultimate release of Diane. He gave full credit to Pat wondering, on reflection, that perhaps the release of Diane was a strange, but comforting, relaxant for Pat.

"I'm more impressed with her the more I hear about her," Lord Stonebridge said.

Carolyn jumped in. "Makes my roles seem rather boring, perhaps?"

"A discussion for another time," he replied standing and walking to the door. "Let's have lunch and return at 1:30. I believe, Miss Andrews, you have arranged a picnic for yourself and our special guest?"

"Yes sir," Carolyn said, smiling at Ed. "A special picnic out on the grounds."

They left for lunch, all in good humour.

Ed carried the picnic basket in one hand, holding hands with Carolyn with the other. She had taken his hand as soon as they had left the manor, making the point that she was not concerned who saw them. It was a clear spring day, flowers were blooming, and the air was filled with birds working on their annual nest-building. They walked without speaking, up through the woods at the far end of the manor grounds and into the centre of the woods; into Carolyn's favourite spot. She took the picnic basket from him, put it on the ground and turned to him.

"I want you to make love to me, Ed. Right here and right now."

He looked around, wary of who could see. "Are you sure, Carolyn? I er . . ."

"What am I wearing, Ed?"

"A lovely summer dress."

"Where are the buttons, Ed?"

He gulped. "On the front."

"My bra hooks up at the front, Ed, and there are two blankets in the basket. Any more questions, Ed?"

He smiled and took her into his arms. "God I love you, Carolyn." He kissed her lips gently and then pressed his body hard to her to feel her wonderful touch. He whispered in her ear. "Are you wearing panties, Carolyn?"

"That," she grinned, pointing to the picnic basket, "is for me to know . . ."

"Yes, yes, yes," he said, unbuttoning her dress, "and for me to find out!"

"That was wonderful, Ed." Carolyn fastened the top button of her dress. "This is now *our* special spot, and that can never change." She looked over to him smiling. "C'mon it's time to eat."

Ed watched her arrange the food, knowing that this had been a special spot for Carolyn and her childhood boyfriend Paul Reynolds, the son of Lady Stonebridge's best friend, Lady Reynolds. It was here they had agreed to get married, although at the time they had been only eight years old. Ed wondered if he should have a feeling of being used by Carolyn. Was their lovemaking a way for her to break from the past? He considered the question, but quickly put it out of his mind. It didn't matter. He loved Carolyn as deeply as he could love anyone.

Carolyn poured the tea from the flask and handed Ed a cup.

"To us," she toasted, raising her cup.

"To us," Ed agreed, "but mostly to the most amazing and beautiful person in the world—Miss Andrews."

"I love it when you call me that, Ed."

"Yes I know," he smiled.

"And I don't say it often, Ed, but I do love you and always will."

He leaned over, kissed her forehead and grabbed a sandwich as he sat back. "Let's eat," he said. "Being with you makes me hungry."

"For what?" she asked, winking.

"First for you, and only then for food."

Carolyn poured them some more tea. "Would you like me to tell you about my visit to Number 10?" she asked excitedly.

"Yes, of course. I totally forgot all about it. Tell me what you can."

"Well," Carolyn said, picking up her cup of tea and extending her little finger for show, "it really was an exciting experience. Mrs. Thatcher was such a charming hostess. She knew of all the details of course, but she spoke in a way that skirted the unseemly parts. She asked how I was without mentioning the kidnapping attempt, and she made reference to 'our Canadian resident'—that's you, Ed—being in fine health. She had spoken with Prime Minister Mulroney just that morning. I was so proud of you I wanted to tell her what a super person you are, but . . ." She shrugged. "To be honest, I was too scared to speak. It was all over in ten minutes, but I'll never forget it. Goodness, I think I'll vote for her next time!"

"No photos?" Ed asked.

"None allowed."

"I'm proud of you, Carolyn. Makes the job all seem worth the risk eh?"

Carolyn nodded enthusiastically. "Yes it does, Ed, it really does."

They finished their picnic and after a slow walk back, identifying four birds on the way, they were back in Lord Stonebridge's office a few minutes early.

Lord Stonebridge looked at his watch. "You're early, well done," he said.

"Usually early, rarely late," Ed replied, taking his seat.

"Perhaps you could pass on that piece of wisdom to Lady Stonebridge," Lord Stonebridge suggested.

Mr. Cooper entered the room and closed the door. "Lady Stonebridge has asked me to announce that she has invited Lord and Lady Reynolds for dinner tonight." He kept his expression flat, and took his seat.

Carolyn almost left her seat, but instead looked furiously at her father, Lord Stonebridge.

"She is your mother's best friend," Lord Stonebridge said, in a rare reference to the family line. "Besides," he added, looking at Carolyn, "they haven't seen you in quite a while have they?" He didn't wait for an answer; the question was strictly hypothetical. He then spoke to everyone. "So let's turn to the business at hand shall we?"

Ed looked over at Carolyn and smiled. In return Carolyn rolled her eyes and shook her head in apology.

Lord Stonebridge continued. "Miss Andrews and I met with the prime minister last week and an update on that brief but important meeting is as good a starting point as any." He took a deep breath. "It's fair to say she pulled a King Henry on me."

Carolyn nodded her understanding.

Mr. Cooper looked puzzled.

"Sorry, sir, you've lost me on that one," Ed said.

"'Who will rid me of this man . . .'" Lord Stonebridge quoted.

"Henry the second; Thomas Beckett," Carolyn added.

"Got it," Ed said, thoughtfully. "Does she really want him dead?"

They were all aware the discussion was about Patrick Magee, the known IRA member responsible for the Brighton Bombing. With five people dead and thirty-four injured, it had been a vicious attack on the British Cabinet, and an attack that still created division between Irish and English neighbours.

"She may want him dead," Lord Stonebridge replied, "but that is not going to be our goal or expectation. We want to bring him back to British justice. We want him very much alive."

"We, sir?" Ed asked.

"Yes we," Lord Stonebridge answered abruptly.

"Yes, sir," Ed said, regretting his question.

"What Lord Stonebridge is referring to," Mr. Cooper said interceding "is that both Houses have active Committees looking at national security issues, and it is Parliament that provides input and over-sight into the day-to-day activities of the Department, not just the prime minister."

"Well put, General, and I apologise for my curtness, Mr. Crowe."

"So the goal then is simple," Carolyn added, bringing the discussion to a head, "we want Mr. Magee back on British soil and then we want him arrested."

"Succinct and accurate," Lord Stonebridge said. "And before you ask, we are not sure where he is. We do know he left for Europe before the bombing, so we can assume he is still at-large safely out of the country. Our direction is clear, we want him back on British soil and we are not going to wait for months sorting out repatriation laws from the country where we find him. And find him we will. It is my number one responsibility. It is the Department's number one responsibility. We have our most knowledgeable people working on this. We have increased our network of contacts. It is just a matter of time. Our work here is done."

"That is excellent, sir," Mr. Cooper said. "Then there is no need to delay Eddie any longer. He can return to Canada, knowing that things are well in hand. And if I may, Miss Andrews, you can now safely return to Paris and enjoy the wonders of springtime in Paris."

"Absolutely," Lord Stonebridge said, spreading both hands on his desk. "Absolutely!"

"Hold you horses here," Carolyn interrupted. "I'm on the special task force searching for our Mr. Magee, and I have no intention of giving this a pass. I've met him, spoken to him, and he's threatened to kidnap me. I'm in and that's final." She paused. "If you agree, sir," she added quietly.

Lord Stonebridge looked at Mr. Cooper, and shrugged. "What can I say, General, she does make a good point."

"Excuse me, sir," Ed said, standing, "but I've also . . ."

"Yes, yes, Mr. Crowe," Lord Stonebridge said, waving him to sit, "you've also met him and spoken to him; you're in!"

Ed sat, trying not to grin. "Thank you, sir."

Mr. Cooper took a deep breath and shook his head. "Never let it be said . . ." He didn't finish the sentence. His point was made. He chuckled inwardly. He wouldn't have expected any different reaction. He was proud of both of them.

The four of them worked out the outline for a plan, the details of which would depend on which country Pat Magee was in when they located him. It was clear in everyone's mind that it was *when* they located him, not *if*.

"So I am overall lead," Lord Stonebridge said, as they wrapped up the afternoon. "The General will work closely with me since he knows more about European countries than any of us. Miss Andrews will communicate with CSIS through Miss Weston. Miss Weston will lead in Canada and communicate the progress directly to Mr. Crowe. Any questions?"

There were none. They had agreed on the idea of having Canadians responsible for encouraging, the gentle word they used instead of forcing, Pat Magee back to British soil was 'brilliant'. While not directly stated but implied was the benefit of having Carolyn deal directly with Pat. This clearly addressed the too-close-for-business friendship that existed between Carolyn and Ed.

"Then, Miss Andrews," Lord Stonebridge said, wrapping up the meeting, "why don't you set up Mr. Crowe in the Aylesbury bedroom, and let's all meet for a pre-dinner glass of wine in twenty minutes. No doubt Lord and Lady Reynolds will not be late." He smiled as he left the room.

"Yikes," Ed said, looking around the bedroom. "This is almost as big as my mum's main floor. You could have a party in here."

The bedroom was on the second floor of Stonebridge Manor, down the hall from Lord Stonebridge's office. It was a corner room, with large windows facing both the back and the west side of the manor. Carolyn opened the windows to let in the fresh air. Ed bounced on the bed. It was a four-poster and undoubtedly a valuable antique. He fell backwards spread-eagle and then sat up taking in all of the surroundings.

"If my mum sleeps in this room, she'll never fall asleep," he said. "She'll want to stay awake just to enjoy the feeling."

"Then I'll make sure she sleeps here," Carolyn smiled, "and I'll make sure she's not woken until late." She walked toward the door. "I'll see you downstairs."

"Hold on," Ed said, catching up to her. "What am I supposed to say to Lord and Lady Reynolds? They probably blame me for your breaking off with their son. Jesus, this could be scary."

"Don't be silly, Ed. They're just nice people who want to see me, and I don't doubt want to see who you are too. Just slip on your tux, and I'll see you downstairs."

"Oh God," Ed groaned. "They won't be in formal dress will they? I don't even have a tie."

Carolyn smiled. "No, I'm just kidding. Just wash-up and I'll see you downstairs in ten." She quickly kissed him, squeezed his hands, and left him to get ready.

Five minutes later there was a knock on his door. Ed ran to open it, expecting Carolyn. It was the maid holding a dark blue tie, which she offered to Ed. "Courtesy of Lord Stonebridge, sir," she said, and slipped away.

The tie didn't match his jacket very well, but it was a relief to have a tie to cover his otherwise casual attire. He put a Windsor knot in the tie, knowing this would go down better with the older men who would be more formally dressed. As he got closer he heard chatter and laughter in the Library. Taking a deep breath and straightening his back, as his mother always told him to, he walked to the Library.

He maintained the smile, but his heart sank to his stomach. Lord Reynolds was wearing a tux, and his height and size made him the dominant figure in the room. Lady Reynolds wore a long evening dress with a variety of jewellery that set the dress off wonderfully. Lord Stonebridge and Mr. Cooper wore business suits, while Carolyn and her mother wore shorter cocktail dresses than Lady Reynolds. Ed might as well have been wearing a lumberjack outfit.

"Ah, Mr. Crowe," Lady Stonebridge exclaimed, catching Ed by his arm and walking him into the room. Ed smiled at those he knew, and turned to meet the enemy.

"Lord and Lady Reynolds," Lady Stonebridge said, "it is a pleasure to introduce you to Mr. Crowe. Mr. Crowe is a Londoner like myself, and now lives in Canada."

Ed shook their hands, hoping his was not too sweaty to be noticed.

"And how is your new prime minister?" Lord Reynolds asked in a deep and friendly voice. As Lord Reynolds's asked the question Carolyn handed Ed a glass of white wine. It was a great comfort to have her standing by his side. He appreciated the support.

"Well, sir," Ed said, relaxed by Carolyn's closeness, "I think the jury is still out on Mr. Mulroney. He is certainly more business-friendly. Perhaps I could contact you and let you have my final opinion once it is fully formed."

Lady Stonebridge's eyes were now wide open, and her jaw dropped just a touch.

Lord Reynolds's laughed very loud and threw back his head. "Excellent, Mr. Crowe, an excellent answer." He reached into his pocket. "Here's my card, please let me know your final analysis." He was still laughing as he walked past Ed to talk with Lord Stonebridge. Ed slipped the card into his pocket without looking at it.

"So tell me, Mr. Crowe," Lady Reynolds's enquired, "I understand it gets very cold in Canada. Is that so?"

Ed was about to respond 'Brass monkey', the colloquial expression for 'cold enough to freeze the balls off a brass money', but Carolyn's soft kick on his foot changed that.

"Yes, it does get very cold, ma'am, but Canadians have a clever way of working around the cold."

"Really?" Lady Reynolds asked. "What clever trick do they do then?"

"They turn up the thermostat."

"Everyone?" she asked, surprised at the answer.

"Yes, ma'am. Everyone has central heating. No winters of discontent across the pond, Lady Reynolds."

The conversation was ended by a call to the table by the maid. Ed and Carolyn followed Lady Reynolds into the dining room. Carolyn grabbed Ed's hand briefly and squeezed gently. He felt the confidence build in him aided by her support. He turned to her and smiled. "You look very charming this evening, Miss Andrews." He spoke quite formally.

"Why thank you, Mr. Crowe," she replied. "How nice of you to notice. And that is such a fine tie you have on. It looks like it may have been purchased at Harrods."

"It may well have," Ed replied, feeling the quality of tie. "I confess I don't now recall where it was purchased."

They took their seats. Ed was seated next to Carolyn, directly across from Lord and Lady Reynolds. Lady Stonebridge had set the stage for an ongoing conversation.

The soup was served and the conversation was limited to weather and politics. Lord Reynolds was obviously dyed-in-the wool Conservative and his wife seemed to go along with his point of view. It was quickly apparent that Carolyn was the only one expressing any point of view other than in favour of Mrs. Thatcher, although Ed knew that her recent visit with Mrs. Thatcher had helped soften her perspective somewhat.

"How could such a nice young lady such as you, Carolyn, lean toward a socialist perspective?" Lady Reynolds asked politely.

"I'm not so sure, Lady Reynolds," Carolyn responded, "that providing school milk to children, especially poor children, is so anti-capitalistic that Mrs, Thatcher had to eliminate it when she was Education Secretary in the seventies. Why my own mother was raised on school milk, and surely she did not suffer from it?"

Lady Stonebridge smiled and sipped her wine. She was not going to get dragged into the discussion.

"And surely, Lady Reynolds," Carolyn continued, "it could not be so bad if a few children from more wealthy families enjoyed the benefit of milk. Indeed, would eliminating the milk not have cost farming jobs and reduced the profit of the dairies that produced the milk? Surely both farmers and dairy owners were likely members of the Conservative party. So then who won on the deal?"

"But that cannot be compared to the wholesale nationalization of so many industries that occurred during the time of the Labour Government following the war, can it?" Lady Reynolds asked.

"No, it cannot. I agree," Carolyn added. "But my point is that decisions should be based on the good of the country as whole and not just on political doctrines. I have no more respect for a single-minded union leader, than I do for an industrialist that cares little about the health and living standards of his workers."

"I see your point, Carolyn," Lady Reynolds said, "and I will bear that in mind as an interesting point of view."

Ed sipped his wine and kicked Carolyn's foot under the table.

Knowing that she had to raise the question, Carolyn asked how Paul was doing.

"Ah yes," Lady Reynolds said, "he is doing very well, and is soon to be promoted to partner in the firm. I don't wish to sound overly motherly, but we are both very proud of him."

"Please say hello from me," Carolyn asked.

"I will certainly do that," Lady Reynolds answered with a smile.

The main course was venison, which to his surprise Ed quite enjoyed. The remainder of the conversation was limited to items of general interest, and he felt almost comfortable.

"Now that wasn't so bad was it?" Lady Stonebridge queried. The Reynolds had left, and the five of them were sipping on the last of the wine in the library.

"Most enjoyable, Mother," Carolyn said. "And what was the jury's decision?"

"What do you mean, my dear?" Lady Stonebridge asked.

"What I mean, Mother, is what comments were passed between yourself and Lady Reynolds about our guest Mr. Crowe?"

Ed acted as if he wasn't there, which seemed to befit the circumstance.

"Well, as I recall," Lady Stonebridge said, appearing to be thinking back weeks not minutes, "both Lord and Lady Reynolds were quite taken with Mr. Crowe. They seemed impressed with what Lord Reynolds called 'his intelligent subtlety'."

"I see," said Carolyn, "and here I was thinking they were impressed with his Harrods tie."

Ed looked down on the tie he had borrowed. "Is it really from Harrods?" he asked.

"All seventy pounds of it," Lord Stonebridge said. "But before you jump to any conclusions, Mr. Crowe, please have a look at Lord Reynolds business card."

Ed looked at the card. It read 'Lord Paul Richard Reynolds, Company Director, London, England.' "Very nice," Ed said, not sure of the implications.

"He is a member of the board of Harrods," Mr. Cooper added. "And as we speak the company is in final discussions to be purchased by the Fayed brothers."

"Egyptians." Lady Stonebridge spoke curtly.

"Ah, the free enterprise system working at its best," Carolyn felt she had to contribute.

"Touché," Lord Stonebridge said, finishing his wine. "I'm done for the night. Long day tomorrow."

Carolyn walked Ed to his bedroom, kissed him gently, winked, and left for her room.

Feeling somewhat awkward sleeping in the nude in such a grand bedroom, Ed closed the curtains except on the east side. He was looking forward to seeing the sun shine through the luxurious windows. He fell asleep quickly.

He felt his nose being touched and he woke smiling, knowing it was Carolyn. The room was dark with the moon shedding a large sliver of light through the east window. Carolyn sat on the side of the bed. She was wearing a long silk nightgown. She smelled wonderful. Ed sat up, took her hand and kissed it gently.

"You look beautiful," he murmured.

She smiled at the comment. "Thank you, Ed. You did very well this evening. I know it's not my place to say so, but I was very proud of you."

"Can we make love?" he asked, squeezing her hand.

"No, Ed. We need to talk. Or more to the point, I need to ask you a few questions."

He sat up straighter. "Fire away. Did I get food on the tie?"

"No, Ed. It's about Pat."

He was tempted to let go of her hand, but she held it tight.

"Business?" he asked.

"Sort of." She held his hand tighter. "When she visited you the day after the shooting—in the evening . . ."

"For food and wine," Ed clarified.

"Yes, for food and wine. Did she . . ."

"She didn't eat much or drink too much wine," Ed interrupted.

"I'm sure she didn't." Carolyn said, speaking slowly. "Did she sleep over?"

Ed gulped and licked his lips. "Wow, I didn't expect that. Should you ask such a question, Carolyn?"

"Yes, I should."

He took a deep breath. "No she did not sleep over, as you put it. She drove to her parent's place, although I was worried about her driving. She was still rather shaken."

"Did you send her flowers?"

"No. She's not a flowers type of lady."

Carolyn let go of his hand. "What do you mean? All ladies are flower types of ladies. She saved your life, and you didn't send her flowers?" She was speaking louder to make her point.

"You're confusing me, Carolyn," Ed said. "You know I love you and you know I'm going to ask you to marry me in less than five years . . ."

"One thousand-six-hundred-and-eighty days," she added for clarity.

"Okay, I'm sure your math is correct, being an Oxford grad and all. But . . ."

"Ed, let me make myself clear without getting into too much detail. I love you. I like Pat a lot. I believe you like Pat a great deal. I know that Pat loves you. We now have to work together. Ed, I want it to work. I don't want you making decisions and suggestions based on personal feelings. Am I making myself clear?"

"I think so," Ed managed.

"Would you like to ask me about my, shall we say, personal life?"

"God no, Carolyn, and please don't tell me. Christ you'd break my heart if you told me . . . Oh God!"

She took his hand, kissed it and held it tight. "If I get pregnant in the next five years, Ed, and I have no plans to do so, there is no doubt that you will be the father. Is that clear enough for a secondary school educated gentleman?"

"Clear enough for this bloke," Ed said, taking a deep breath of contentment. "You are amazing, Miss Andrews. I love you so much."

"I know you do, Ed, and I love it when you call me that. Now move over and let me snuggle up. Just snuggle okay?"

"Nothing else on my mind," he lied, and he held her as tightly as he could.

"So summarize please," Carolyn asked as they lay in each other's arms.

"You'll make sure I'm not a father in England . . ." he said slowly.

"And?"

"And I'll make sure I'm not a father, shall we say, on a more international basis."

"Yes, we shall say that," Carolyn agreed as she slipped out of the bed. "More importantly, and this is my main point, when and if the three of us do work together, then it will be strictly business. No personal issues, full stop. And that's an order. I'll see you in the morning." She leaned down, kissed his forehead and quickly left the room.

Ed rolled over, knowing who the boss was. No surprise there.

CHAPTER TEN

SATURDAY MARCH 23RD, 1985

• • • ● ● ● •

C arolyn turned the Jag. off the A4010 and joined the A40 heading toward London. The traffic was heavy, it was always heavy, but they moved at an acceptable speed for a Saturday. They had declined breakfast, knowing that Ed's mother would be arranging lunch for them and Roy Johnson.

"So what are you going to say to Roy?" Ed asked. Roy had asked for Carolyn's hand in marriage the first time he met her. She knew, Ed knew, and Roy knew, that it was intended to be a significant compliment to Carolyn, not a true offer of marriage. Ed also knew that if the impossible happened, and Carolyn said yes, Roy would be only too happy to proceed.

"You can't ask me that," Carolyn replied, keeping her eyes on the road.

"Hey, if you can ask me if a lady friend slept over, I can ask you if you're going to say yes to a marriage proposal."

She smiled. "Yes, of course you can. It's just that I'm not going to answer you."

"Would I be Best Man?"

"Nice weather today."

"Will you love, honour, and obey?"

She looked at him out of the corner of her eye. "When, or should I say if, I ever get married, Mr. Crowe, I will love, honour—as in respect—and share responsibility for a happy marriage."

"Good answer, Miss Andrews. If you do say yes to Roy, I'll pass on your suggested wording. Might it be a church wedding?"

She grinned slyly. "You keep talking about my marrying Roy, and the idea sounds better and better as we speak!"

"Nice weather today," he said quickly and decisively.

Mrs. Crowe was full of excitement as she ushered Carolyn into the living room. "Roy is already here, Miss Andrews. He's done nothing but talk about seeing you again." Ed followed behind carrying his bag.

Roy stood as Carolyn entered the room. They hugged and sat across from each other in the only two soft chairs in the room. Mrs Crowe went into the kitchen to put on a fresh pot of tea. Ed stood at the door smiling. He was happy to be home and greeted exactly as he had expected.

Roy broke off his conversation with Carolyn, stood and walked over to Ed. They shook hands as childhood friends were inclined to do—firmly and genuinely.

"Good to see you, Eddie," Roy said. "Always a pleasure. Especially when you bring Carolyn along with you."

"Yes, I'd noticed," Ed nodded. "Good to see you, Roy."

Mrs Crowe joined them with the mandatory pot of tea. "Here we go," she added. "Let's have a nice cuppa."

"Could I perhaps see Roy privately?" Carolyn asked, standing and taking Roy's hand. "If you'd excuse us for a moment?" She and Roy walked through the kitchen into the back garden. Ed and his mother could see but not hear them.

"Oh, that's so beautiful," Mrs. Crowe snivelled, wiping her eyes. "She is such a nice girl. I do hope she says yes."

"You what?" Ed exclaimed.

His mother sat straight and looked at Ed. "Well if you won't ask her to marry *you*, all the more fool you. At least Roy had the gumption to ask!"

Ed rolled his eyes. "Yes, Mother."

Mrs. Crowe poured the tea to keep herself busy as Carolyn and Roy returned to their seats. She handed them each a cup, her hands shaking slightly.

Roy took a sip of tea and broke the silence. "You'll be happy to know that in answer to my request for her hand in marriage, Carolyn has . . ." he took a further sip of tea as Mrs Crowe couldn't take her eyes from him, ". . . Carolyn has indicated, in a most charming manner, that she is unable to say yes."

"Oh my," Mrs Crowe sighed. "That is so nice. *Unable to say yes.* Isn't that nice, Edwin?" She dabbed her eyes.

"A most charming response," Ed agreed. "It is heart-warming to see my two best friends get along so well."

Mrs. Crowe broke down in tears and ran into the kitchen. Carolyn quickly followed her, seizing a napkin from the tea tray as she did.

"One of these days, Eddie, my boy," Roy said. "One of these days!"

Ed raised his right hand. "I promise."

"*Now a promise made is a debt unpaid . . .*" Roy quoted. "Robert Service. Another limey that did well in Canada."

"*There are strange things done in the midnight sun . . .*" Ed added. They shook hands.

Ed's mother and Carolyn came back in the room just like old friends. Mrs Crowe was jovial and acting as if nothing had happened. She sat down and picked up her cup of tea. "Carolyn's parents have invited me out to their place in the country," she announced smiling. "The next time Carolyn comes in from Paris she is going to pick me up and drive me out to meet her parents." She smiled broadly.

"Very nice Mrs. C.," Roy said genuinely happy for her. "And here I was hoping it would be me."

Mrs. Crowe held her head smugly in the air. "I'll tell you all about it, Roy, when I return. Carolyn also told me that her mother is fond of Edwin. That's nice too."

"She's quite a lady, Mum," Ed said, smiling at his own play on words. "And she's from Neasden. Just up the road a bit."

"We'll all have a great time, Mrs. Crowe," Carolyn interjected. "Nice for you to get a bit of the country air."

"Oh, I am so looking forward to it," Mrs. Crowe added. She left for the kitchen to organize lunch.

"Something's going on here," Roy pondered, rubbing his chin. "What aren't you telling me?" He had been listening to the conversation and his strong level of intuition had been aroused.

Ed looked at Carolyn to respond. She motioned back to Ed.

"Well," Ed said slowly, dragging out his thoughts as he spoke, "let's say my bedroom last night is about the same size as the main floor of this house."

"I knew it!" Roy trumpeted. "I felt it in my veins. It's not an old thatched cottage your parents own; it's a bloody mansion isn't it?"

Carolyn put her finger to her mouth. "Not so much a mansion as a manor."

"A manor with a small M or a big M?" he queried, now enjoying the game.

"Big," Ed whispered.

Roy looked at Carolyn. "I'm listening."

"Stonebridge Manor," Carolyn conceded.

Roy looked at Carolyn and then at Ed. "As in Lord Stonebridge? As in the gentleman the press are all over regarding last year's Brighton Bombing? As in the Head of MI6?"

Carolyn nodded. "Please don't say anything to Mrs. Crowe, Roy. I'll explain it all as I drive her there."

Roy's eyes rolled to the top of his head. "No problem there, Carolyn. My lips are sealed." He turned to Ed. "You, however, have a lot more explaining to do than I ever thought."

Ed raised his right hand. "Promise." He lowered his hand just as his mother came back into the room with lunch.

Mrs Crowe had made a large toad-in-the-hole, one of Ed's favourite meals. Roy, being the eldest male in the room, proceeded to cut and serve.

Roy placed a slice on Carolyn's plate. "Don't get this in Paris, do you, Carolyn?"

"Not a chance," she replied. "Makes me glad I'm back home for a good solid meal."

Mrs Crowe enjoyed the compliment.

Ed thought back to the exact same meal he had cooked for Pat, and to the venison from last night's meal at Stonebridge Manor. He preferred the meal in front of him, and tucked in.

Mrs. Crowe looked at Carolyn. "So I notice, Carolyn, that while you were in North America you didn't pick up the habit of eating with just a fork?"

"No I managed to avoid that one," Carolyn replied, keeping her eyes away from Ed.

With his head down Ed quickly and quietly moved his fork from his right hand to his left, and picked up his knife.

After lunch was served and the table cleared away, Carolyn said her goodbyes receiving big hugs from Mrs. Crowe and Roy. Ed walked her to her car.

Ed took her hands in his. "Me thinks my mum has you walking on water."

Carolyn smiled. "She is a wonderful lady. I am so looking forward to introducing her to my parents."

Ed reached into his wallet and gave Carolyn a twenty and a ten-pound note. "Would you buy her something from me for her to wear for dinner? I want it to be special for her."

Carolyn took the notes. "I'll make sure she looks terrific, Ed, and it won't be Marks and Sparks."

They held each other tight, kissed quickly and Carolyn got into the car. "So I'll see you when I see you, Ed. Let's hope that's soon—both personally and professionally."

"I'm looking forward to it," Ed smiled.

"And send Pat some flowers for God's sake."

"I will do that as soon as I get back."

"I love you, Ed."

Ed gulped, holding back his emotions, "I love you, Carolyn."

Carolyn waved and drove away.

Ed watched the car drive to the end of the street and turn right. He took several deep breaths to compose himself and walked back into the house.

Mrs Crowe and Roy were relaxing with yet another pot of tea. Ed thought about pouring himself a cup, but decided against it.

Mrs. Crowe put down her cup. "She's a very lovely young lady."

Ed nodded in agreement. Roy toasted the remark with his cup of tea.

"Well, Edwin," she continued, "don't you have anything to say about her? She's your friend."

Ed sat down, deciding to pour himself a cup of tea to give him time to think. "She picked me up at the airport, I stayed at her house in the country, and she drove me here today. If you didn't peek outside when she left, I kissed her goodbye. She invited you to meet her parents, which I know you'll enjoy. And, sadly perhaps, she couldn't say yes to Roy's offer of marriage."

"So what's your point, Eddie?" Roy asked, hoping to help his friend's ramblings.

Ed rolled his eyes and shrugged. "I don't want to ask a question of Carolyn unless I know in my heart of hearts that she would answer yes. Let's chat after you've visited her parents, Mum. I think you'll understand more."

Mrs. Crowe squinted in a questioning manner.

Roy helped out. "That's a grand idea, Eddie. So for now let's agree she is a real gem and part of the family—so to speak."

Mrs. Crowe accepted the compromise. "I'll phone you as soon as I get back from meeting her parents, Edwin. You've always had good common sense and there's no reason to suggest otherwise now. More tea anyone?"

Before either could respond there was a rapid and heavy knock at the front door. Ed walked quickly to open it. Carolyn stood there obviously agitated.

"Ed, grab your bag, you have to come with me. Now please!"

Ed stepped back. "What do I tell . . . ?"

"Tell them anything. Tell them we're running away. Tell them we're eloping. Ed, please do as your told." She raised her hand to slow things down. "Please do as I ask, Ed."

He partially closed the door, went inside and was back in thirty seconds with his bag. "Okay, let's go."

Carolyn drove as fast as she could without creating accidents. She was headed north. Ed knew they were heading back to Stonebridge Manor. He waited for Carolyn to speak.

"I got a call on my mobile," she said speaking as calmly as she could, keeping her eyes on the traffic ahead.

Ed nodded.

Neither spoke for the thirty-five minutes that it took them to get out of London and onto the M40 heading north-west.

"You're speeding," Ed said quietly.

Carolyn slowed down to only ten miles an hour over the speed limit. "Thanks," she replied, quickly touching his hand. "It's urgent."

"Really? Who'd have guessed?"

It wasn't until they were on the A4010, that Carolyn had to slow down to the allowed speed. They were now in the true English countryside and the roads were narrow and winding.

Ed looked at Carolyn. "Can you tell me?"

She shook her head. "No. I have my orders. Sorry."

"Okay," he shrugged. "I still love you."

Carolyn smiled, shaking her head slightly in mild disbelief. Her smiled slipped away as she drove into Stonebridge Manor grounds. She knew this was going to be difficult.

There was no Lady Stonebridge to meet them at the front door as was often the case. Having left the manor only hours before, Lady Stonebridge's no-show was a message. Carolyn led him directly up to Lord Stonebridge's office.

Lord Stonebridge and the General were standing at Stonebridge's large desk looking seriously at what was on the desk. They sat as Ed and Carolyn entered. Lord Stonebridge looked worried as he gestured for a now nervous Ed and Carolyn to sit.

Lord Stonebridge laid his hands on his desk. "Your mother is fine, Ed." It wasn't a question, it was a statement. "But we need to talk."

Ed shook his head totally confused. "I . . . er . . . we just left my mother an hour ago. I don't . . ."

Lord Stonebridge raised his hand. "Let me explain, Mr. Crowe, let me explain." He pointed at his desk. "An envelope arrived for you this morning at your office, delivered by hand. Thank goodness Diane opened it. She was, is, still uncertain about what happened recently at the agency. When she saw what the envelope contained, she immediately phoned Pat Weston in Ottawa who, by the grace of God, was working on a Saturday. I have in front of me a faxed copy of the enclosure, front and back, courtesy of the Halton Police department and Miss Weston's perseverance." He beckoned Ed and Carolyn to his desk.

Ed almost stumbled in getting to the desk. He looked down not believing what he was seeing. "That's my mum," he muttered "What the hell . . ?" On the desk was copy of an 8X10 photo.

"Where's it taken at, Ed?" Carolyn asked.

"At the grocer in Kensal Rise," Mr. Cooper said. "Just up the street from Ed's mother's home." In the photo Mrs. Crowe was looking over vegetables on the inside of the grocer's apparently talking to someone not in the photo.

Ed looked at Lord Stonebridge, nodding his head to see the reverse side of the photo.

On the back of the photo in block lettering it read:

WE WANT OUR MAN BACK, AND ALL WILL BE FINE. WE WILL BE IN TOUCH.

Ed stumbled back into his chair. "Fucking hell," he gasped.

Carolyn couldn't believe what she had heard.

"Fucking hell, indeed," Lord Stonebridge agreed.

Carolyn sat down in dismay at the language. She looked at Mr. Cooper for guidance.

Mr. Cooper nodded. "Ditto!" he shouted.

In a moment she would remember for the rest of her life, all three looked at her for comment. She sat straight in the chair. "Okay! Effing hell it is."

Lord Stonebridge spread his large hands across his desk and looked around the room. "Well that's settled then. We're all in agreement on that one. The photo is on its way here, and will be delivered early tomorrow morning. Perhaps, General, you'd be good enough to update Mr. Crowe and Miss Andrews on our activities since we requested their attendance here today."

Mr Cooper spoke clearly and to the point. "First an up-date from Miss Weston in Ottawa. The photo was taken with a very expensive and up-to-date camera. While it cannot be obvious on the faxed copy, the photo was taken from outside the grocer's store with a telephoto lens. On the photo it clearly identifies reflections on the window, not seen by our copy. The camera speed was very fast. As you can see the image of Mrs. Crowe is most precise with the background less clear. Given that she is moving at the time tells us that the photo was taken by either a professional photographer or a very qualified amateur. We suspect the former."

"Any fingerprints?" Carolyn asked.

"Just a couple of Diane Cooke's," Mr. Cooper continued, "the rest have been wiped clean. Now as Eddie likely knows there are just two professional photographers in the Kensal Rise area. I rang them up today and the two of you have appointments with both of them tomorrow." He raised one eyebrow. "I afraid I had to lie to them to get Sunday appointments. I told them you're getting married and . . . well, you need a photographer. Sorry about that."

Carolyn laughed. "And just today I declined an offer of marriage."

Lord Stonebridge couldn't believe what he was hearing. "You what? You . . . who?" was all he could manage.

"Oh, don't worry it wasn't Ed that I said 'no' to, it was his best friend." She waved off any further discussion. "I'll explain later. It was personal."

Mr. Cooper continued. "The appointments are at nine and eleven tomorrow morning. This allows Eddie time to catch his flight back to Canada if that is still in the cards." He looked around for questions. Everyone was onside. "Now two other things have been arranged. Mrs. Poplowski, Ed's mum's neighbour, is looking for a lodger, and as of tomorrow she'll have one. He's one of ours of course, but no names please. Secondly there is a new park attendant at Queen's Park whose responsibility is to manage the new ornamental garden which conveniently is immediately across the street from Mrs. Crowe. She's ours of course. No names."

Lord Stonebridge took over. "So what we have is visual contact both day and night. Having said that, Mr. Crowe, we do not expect any contact by the IRA with your mother, but that's not the point here. Her safety is priority. We certainly expect they will contact you as they have said. We do not, however, expect that to be too soon. They'll want you to worry. I want you *not* to worry."

Ed spoke firmly. "Thank you, sir. I do appreciate your direct involvement."

Carolyn took the opportunity to calm the atmosphere. "So, Ed, what did you tell your mother and Roy about leaving so quickly?"

He laughed, thinking back to their reaction. "I told them we were going walk-about."

"And?" Carolyn asked.

"Mum said that was so lovely, and Roy said we have to talk sometime. I'm beginning to think that nothing I do nowadays surprises them."

"That's the spirit," Lord Stonebridge said, and picked up the phone to order a pot of tea.

When the tea was rolled in, along with some digestive biscuits, it was down to work on their plan for the next few weeks, given the new and now disturbing circumstances.

Carolyn dropped Ed off at the local Inn, used only by members and guests of MI6. It was just after 10 pm

"Can you not come in for a brief visit?" Ed asked.

Carolyn shook her head. "I know what your brief visits turn into," she smiled. "I'll see you in the morning. Get a good night's sleep."

Twenty minutes later there was a gentle knock on his door. Carolyn quickly stepped in his room closing the door quietly behind her.

"Let's forget about a 'brief' visit," she said unbuttoning her blouse. "Let's talk about a 'smalls' visit shall we?"

Ed watched in pleasure as she stripped to her smalls and walked into his arms.

"You finish the job," she whispered.

Ed did as he was ordered.

CHAPTER ELEVEN

SUNDAY, MARCH 24TH 1985

• • • • • • •

E d looked again at the photo understanding how, with expert input, you could determine that it was taken through a window. Carolyn drove carefully toward London. They had plenty of time to arrive in time for the interviews and had agreed they would see if they could calculate exactly where the photographer was standing when the photo had been taken.

"It is a good picture," Carolyn said, not taking her eyes off the road.

"Isn't what we're about to do illegal?" Ed asked.

She thought for a moment. "Illegal? Probably. Unusual? Not so much."

"Impersonating a police officer isn't unusual? Where are we, the US?"

"God, I hope we haven't slipped that far. Hey, it's just for a couple of hours. Trust the process, Ed." She winked at him. "Just trust me."

"Okay. And yes it is a good snap. Perhaps one day we can show it to her."

"Not in a million years, lover boy."

"Speaking of which," he said, leaning over to kiss her on her cheek, "I truly do love you."

"So you said last night. Several times as I recall."

Ed nodded, recalling their love making. How he wished they could be together forever. He knew that likelihood was slim, probably impossible. He chuckled to himself; his being married to the daughter of Lord and Lady Stonebridge was about as likely as his flying to the moon. In fact his flying to the moon was more a possibility. All he had to do was join the US Air Force, take six years training . . . He rolled his eyes and dropped the ridiculous notion.

"Penny for your thoughts?" Carolyn asked.

"I was just pondering the possibility of joining the US Air Force. What do you think?"

"Are you crazy?" she laughed. "Then I'd never see you, and we'd never spend the kind of time we had together last night. No, you ain't doing that, mister."

"Yes, dear."

"And please don't call me dear."

"Yes, Miss Andrews."

She shivered. "I love it when you call me that."

"There's something about this photo that doesn't seem right," Ed said thoughtfully. "It'll come to me." He looked up just as they turned south on the M40.

"Well that was easy," Carolyn said enthusiastically. "Let's hope the rest of the day goes as well."

They were standing across the street from the grocery shop comparing the angle of the photo. Directly behind them was the entrance to Kensal Rise train station which stood at the top of the railway bridge.

Ed nodded and looked at his watch. "Okay, let's go see our first photographer about our up-coming wedding."

Carolyn made no response except to walk down the bridge to The Rise Camera Shop.

The door opened quickly and they were invited in by a young man, no more than thirty years of age, sporting the required long hair of an artistic type. He introduced himself as Rex King and closing the door behind them directed them into the back of the shop.

"So when's the big day?" he asked.

"Next May," Carolyn replied.

"Not soon enough," Ed added with a loving smile.

"Good planning," King said. "Let me show you some of my work."

Within five minutes there were ten wedding albums spread across the room. Ed and Carolyn quickly peered through a few of them passing on good feedback but knowing they had to get down to business.

Carolyn took the photo of Mrs. Crowe from the envelope. "We were recommended we should find the photographer that took this. Is it one of yours?"

"Nope," King said quickly, almost too quickly. "I don't live in the past."

"Sorry?" Ed asked. "We were told this was taken with a pretty fancy modern camera by a professional."

"Oh, it was. It was taken with a Cannon AE-1, 35mm, SLR, with a telephoto lens, probably at 1/1000th of a second shutter speed."

"Well that sounds rather up-to-date," Carolyn said, obviously confused by the message.

"Ah, but you're not looking at the big picture are you?" King smiled.

Ed snapped his fingers. "That's it! It's in black and white. Everything is in colour nowadays. I knew there was something missing."

King motioned back toward the train station. "Mr. Albert Henry. Over the bridge, down the street, past the pub; he's your man."

They thanked him, saying they would check out the Mr. Henry before they made up their minds. Stopping for a cup of coffee to kill time, Ed decided not to make any comments about weddings or photo albums. At Carolyn's suggestion, they agreed on how they would approach their eleven o'clock interview.

Mr. Albert Henry was older, probably in his fifties or early sixties. They declined the offer of tea and sat around his desk in the front of the shop. The walls were covered with photos covering all kinds of occasions and descriptions: weddings, funerals, children's parties, animal pictures, weather conditions. Ed was particularly taken with four photos taken in Queen's Park, right across from his mum's place, reflecting the four seasons. He looked but said nothing.

Carolyn showed him the photo of Mrs. Crowe.

"Did you take this, sir," she asked.

"I did indeed," he answered with a smile. "I remember it distinctly."

Carolyn continued. "May I ask you . . . ?"

"No, you may not," he interrupted, maintaining his fatherly smile.

Carolyn raised a hand and extracted a Warrant Card from her purse. "Sir, we are with the Metropolitan police and are investigating a crime."

"Very nice, I'm sure. But as far as I know taking photos on the street is not a major infraction, at least not yet in our so-called modern Britain."

Ed leaned forward. "May I ask, sir, if the gentleman that ordered this photo had an Irish accent?"

Mr. Henry rubbed his chin before replying. "Many people in this area of London have Irish accents. Perhaps you're not from around here? And what makes you think it was a gentleman?"

"My mother was born in Ireland," Carolyn lied. "Our concern is directed at, perhaps I could suggest, a small minority of Irish citizens?"

Mr. Henry took time to think. "Perhaps a pot of tea might help?" Not waiting for a response, he walked slowly into the back of the shop and could be heard gathering the peace offering. He returned in five minutes with a large pot of tea, three cups, milk and sugar along with a small plate of biscuits.

"Now where were we?" he asked, indicating for them to help themselves.

"You said you remembered it distinctly?" Carolyn reminded him as Ed poured their tea.

"It was two Wednesday's ago," he began. "He wanted a few photos taken of the street and in particular some of the people going about their daily chores. He was in a rush, so we went to work immediately. The lady in the photo was doing her regular shopping, I imagine, and he wanted one of her. I took twelve photos in total and he needed them to be developed that day. It was the easiest and quickest twenty pounds I've ever made."

"Did he say why the rush?" Ed asked.

Mr. Henry shrugged. "Said something about catching a fast train that evening so as not to miss the boat. He returned to pick up the photos about fourish and paid me in cash. Insisted on taking the negatives, he did. Heck for twenty quid I'd have bought him a beer."

"Can you describe him?" Carolyn asked.

"Well he was sort of nothing special. Forty something. About five-eight, curly reddish hair, well shaved, wore a wind-breaker and carried a small travelling bag. Strong Irish accent as you suggested but like I say, that's normal around these parts."

"Didn't say which train or boat?" Carolyn asked.

"No, afraid not."

"I don't want to put words in your mouth . . ." Ed said carefully.

"Go on then."

"Did he say boat, or could he have said ferry?"

"Yes, you're right on! He did say ferry." He tapped his head. "Getting old, I guess."

Carolyn and Ed finished their tea, thanked him, and got up to leave.

Mr. Henry held the door open for them. "You two not getting married then? You look like a fine young couple."

Carolyn smiled and looked up at Ed. "I don't deserve anyone as special as this young man," she said. "But if we know of anyone getting married, we'll give them your name and number."

Without commenting further on the marriage issue, they walked back to her car for the trip to Heathrow airport.

"Well that was helpful," Carolyn said thoughtfully, "but nothing definite."

"I think that was most definite," Ed said.

Carolyn pulled the car over to the side of the road and turned to Ed. "You know where he was heading? How?"

"Elementary, my dear Watson," he quipped.

"Come on, come on! What did you pick up? This is important."

Ed nodded his understanding. "This is what I heard. The man was heading for a specific train for a ferry. Mr. Henry called it a 'fast' train. I suspect the word was an 'express' train. So where does that leave us?"

Carolyn shook her head in frustration. "Nowhere."

"Amsterdam, Carolyn. He was heading to Amsterdam. There is only one train each evening from Victoria station, leaves about seven thirty. Train to Harwich, ferry to Hoek van Holland, and then a train to Amsterdam. Arrives the next morning."

"Maybe," she said, not wanting to finalize her thoughts.

"It's called the Amsterdam Express," Ed added smugly. "'Fast' means 'express'. Bet on it!"

She threw her arms around him, hugging him. "I do believe you're right. Well done! Good thing you're a travel agent."

"Just to add to the decision making process," Ed continued. "The train-ferry connection could be to Paris, but there are plenty of trains and ferries. No need to catch a specific train."

"You're a genius, Mr. Crowe. Now let me get you back to Canada. I'll bring your thoughts to 'C' and the General as soon as I get back to the manor." It wasn't often that she referred to her father as 'C', but it made the point that this was all business.

She headed for Heathrow not letting the speed limits get in her way. On the West Way as they passed through Park Royal she put her foot further to the floor.

"Hurrying to get rid of me are you?" Ed asked dryly.

She slowed down and reached over to hold his hand. "Sorry, my enthusiasm's getting the better of me. I'm so excited about getting your message to the manor." She squeezed his hand. "I love you, Ed, and always will."

He kissed her hand and then placed it back on the steering wheel. "Let's do this, Carolyn. If everyone agrees with my assumption, why don't you leave a message on my answering machine indicating that 'Paris' is lovely in the spring?"

When he arrived home that evening there was a message from Carolyn. "I'm in Paris and it's lovely in the spring, Ed. And I love you so much."

CHAPTER TWELVE

SATURDAY MARCH 30ᵀᴴ 1985

• • ● ● ● • •

E d put his cup of tea down and walked to the phone in the kitchen.

"Crowe's nest," he answered.

"You noticed it did you?" Pat asked him.

"My neighbours pointed it out. They thought it was rather clever."

"Hi, Ed. How are you doing?"

"Terrific, Pat, and yourself?"

"Never better. I want to thank you for the flowers, Ed. They're beautiful. Two dozen yet. The girls in the office all wanted to know who E.C. is. It had them guessing."

"What did you tell them?"

"Eric Clapton."

Ed laughed aloud. "Eric Clapton? Where did he come from?"

"He was in town recently and I went to see him. Great show. Whatcha doing?"

"I'm in bed, naked."

"Alone?"

"Of course."

"It's ten in the morning for God's sake. What are you doing in bed?"

"Thinking of you."

She chuckled. "I dread to think."

"Where are you, Pat?"

"At my parent's place."

"Really? Just a few miles away then? Can we meet for coffee?"

She didn't answer right away. He was going to ask again, but waited.

"Probably best if we don't."

"Probably best if we did. Strictly business of course. I'll up-date you on my trip to the manor." He knew she would understand that to mean his visit to MI6 to submit his report on the flight issue and the photo incident.

"I got the up-date."

Ed let the silence speak for a while. "I'd like to see you, Pat. Let me buy you a coffee. Tim Hortons—you tell me where."

She appreciated his insistence. "Okay, Tim's in Milton. Twenty minutes."

"I'll be there in fifteen."

"I thought you were still in bed?"

"I lied . . . . Excuse the pun."

"Oh God," she groaned. "First one there buys."

As quickly as he had dressed and driven to Milton, only a short distance north of Oakville, she was there before he was. Two coffees were on the table along with a blueberry muffin that was cut in half. She didn't stand. He bent down, kissed her forehead and sat across from her. She was wearing a white tennis outfit.

"Practising for Wimbledon?" he asked.

"I'm playing tennis with my father at noon. Indoors."

"I don't mean to be too personal, but you look terrific in that outfit and a lot healthier than last time we met." He was referring to the day after the incidents in the airport and at the travel agency. The day after she had shot and killed a man.

"Thanks. I think. Let's go sit in my car."

They took their coffees and walked to Pat's car, which was parked as far away as possible from the stores.

"BMW," he remarked, sipping his coffee. "Must be nice?"

"It's my father's. I still drive the same car."

Ed put his cup in the holder, turning to Pat. "Can I hold your hand?"

"No."

"Please."

"No."

He took her right hand. "I'll read your palm."

She drew her right hand back and replaced it with her left hand. "It's the left hand, Ed, and sometimes you're so full of it."

Ignoring her comments he looked at her left hand, tracing her lines with his finger.

"That tickles," she laughed.

"You were born very young," he commenced without looking up, "in Ontario, Canada . . ."

"Really?" Pat laughed. "You can tell that much already?"

"You'd be surprised what I can tell you about yourself."

"I'm sure. Just be careful."

He looked back down at her hand, holding it gently. "You are very intelligent, university educated. You're very close to your parents, especially your mother. You have a very good career and do an outstanding job. You were recently promoted, which was very well deserved. You're a bit of a loner, but have one very good friend who is particularly fond of you."

She pulled her hand back. "Let's leave it there shall we?"

Ed smiled at her. "I was going to read your love-line."

"It's very short," she replied, picking up her coffee. "Tell me about your trip to Jolly Old."

"I've got to tell you; everyone there is super impressed with you. In addition to the flight issue, the speed that you managed to take action on the photo of my mother was amazing. I'm not sure if you've received the full up-date from the U.K."

"Yes, I have. Good thinking on your part about the Amsterdam connection. I am very impressed."

"You were working on a Saturday?"

"More fun than sitting at home alone, right?"

"What about Robin?" he asked, referring to Pat's cat.

"Yeah, he's okay," she smiled. "Just that he sleeps during the day."

"So we're all on the select 'IRA committee', including you of course. I'm hoping something positive will come from it."

"It should be interesting," Pat responded flatly. "And the official reason I phoned you today is to tell you that the ongoing work is under the name 'Operation Tea Party'. Pretty damn English I'd say."

Ed knew she didn't want to talk further about what had happened on the plane and decided to change the subject. "I'm looking forward to our cruise in June, Pat. I've been shopping for clothes that befit an assistant to a Captain."

She smiled at the thought of their up-coming boat cruise from Ottawa to Oakville. "So am I, Ed. I am really looking forward to that. Imagine the two of us together for four or five days; and no sex!"

"Imagine!" he agreed.

"I gotta go, Ed. Kiss me goodbye."

He leaned over, pulled her toward him and slipped his hands under her top at the back as he kissed her. He spread his hands as widely as he could across her small back. She moved into him, holding him tight.

"Thanks, Ed. I like it when you do that. It makes me feel special."

He kissed her forehead. "You are special Pat. Very special to me."

She waved him off, pushing him gently out of her car. She tried wiping the tears from her eyes without his seeing. She drove away, not looking back.

Ed watched her drive away. He was worried about her: very worried. He was tempted to follow her, but knew she would resent that if he did. She had never mentioned where her parents lived, and that was a clear message. She wanted privacy in her family life. He knew she had a younger sister, but she never spoke of her. He turned and walked to his car.

He was still thinking about Pat's condition as he got out of the elevator and turned to his left. Pat was standing at his apartment door holding a cup of coffee.

"You forgot this," she said, holding up the coffee.

He took the coffee and unlocked the door. "Thanks. Come on in, I'll make us a cup of tea."

She remained at the door. "I just brought you your coffee."

He removed the coffee lid and drank the remaining cold coffee. "I need a cup of tea now." He gently took her arm, guided her into the apartment and closed the door.

Pat spoke first. "I lied to you. I don't have a game of tennis with my father. And I lied to my parents. I told them I have a game of tennis with you."

"Have a seat. I'll put the kettle on."

She shook her head. "It may come as a surprise to you, Ed, but making a cup of tea doesn't resolve all of the world's problems."

"Is that what we're here to discuss?" he asked with a grin.

"I simply came to return your coffee," she lied.

"Then mission accomplished. My mission is to make a cup of tea and listen to what my friend has to say."

"I don't have anything to say, Ed."

"Then we'll drink tea in silence."

Ed made the tea and kept himself busier than he needed to in the kitchen. Pat sat with her arms crossed, determined not to break the silence. She gave in.

"I need to talk, Ed. I think I'm losing it. I can't sleep at night." She lowered her hands to the table and intertwined her fingers nervously.

"What do you want to talk about, Pat?"

She lost her cool. "What the fuck do you think I want to talk about? The weather? World fucking peace?" Holding her head in one hand, she grabbed at her tea and took a gulp.

"Hot enough for you?" he asked, taking a sip.

She looked down at the table, embarrassed. "Yeah, it's fine." Looking up, she tried to smile. "It's bloody hot actually."

They drank their tea slowly and he topped them up.

"You know, Pat," Ed said, "you're a pretty tough cookie and all, but surely you must accept the fact that shooting a man . . ."

"Killing a man," she interrupted.

"That killing a man is not something you can expect to accept as normal and go on with the rest of the day as if nothing ever happened?"

"It's more than that, Ed. I think he was going to drop the detonator when I shot him."

"Go on."

"Well it all happened in a second. I was looking at his face but out of the corner of my eye it seemed that he was letting go of the detonator. His thumb and index finger were relaxing, moving away from the detonator."

Ed nodded, thinking back to what he heard and saw. "Do you recall what he said; I mean exactly?"

"No," she answered shaking her head, "it all happened so quickly. He said something like 'back off' . . . I'm really not sure."

"'Back off from here, or I'll blow the . . .' is what he said Pat."

"Yeah, okay. Something like that"

"Not something like that Pat. Exactly like that."

"Okay, exactly like that."

Ed sat up straight to make a point. "Pat when I took the detonator from his hand, I swear to God he was not holding it loosely. I don't mean 'Dead man's grip' exactly, but it sure as hell wasn't about to fall out of his hand. Now I'd lie for you, Pat, and you know I'd lie for you, but I promise you that is the truth."

"I know you wouldn't lie to me on something as important as this, Ed. Thanks. I feel quite a bit better."

"Good," he said smiling. "Now try this." He rested his elbow on the table and held his index and middle finger up in the air. "Grip them, Pat."

She pulled a face. "Are you getting dirty on me?"

"Grip them please. Dirty comes later." Pat went along with the idea and grabbed his two fingers. "Now hold them like he was holding the detonator, before he moved his thumb and finger."

She saw his point, and held them with her thumb and index finger touching. She didn't wait for the next instruction, holding his fingers tightly with the three other fingers she opened her thumb and index finger.

Ed nodded. "Now do it again, while saying 'I'll blow the . . . ', and we can guess the rest."

She let go of his fingers and took his hand in hers. "I don't have to, Ed. You've made your point very well. He was freeing his thumb to move it up to the detonator button. He *was* going to blow us all to Hell. Christ, the look on his face should have told me that! I just couldn't be sure." She swallowed to catch her emotions. "Now I feel like such a wimp."

"He was a nasty man, Pat; a self-confessed killer," Ed reminded her. "And while you may be many things, a wimp ain't one of them."

"Thanks. Any more tea in the pot?"

"No," he said standing and taking her hand. "Let me take you out for lunch."

"Dressed for tennis?" she laughed.

"Dressed for tennis and looking quite charming; might I say looking sexy?"

"You might say that to a 'tough cookie' as often as you like, Ed. As often as you like."

As they reached the door to the hallway, Pat turned to Ed. "And by the way you can't swear to God, when you don't believe in one. It's a contradiction in terms. But I still believe you."

Ed nodded. "Good point. And by the way Operation Tea Party is not as English as it is American."

"Duhh?" Pat questioned.

"Boston—right?"

"Very clever," Pat said, prodding him in the chest with her finger. "It was just a test. You passed. Are you going to buy me lunch or not?"

Ed opened the door and they left for lunch.

CHAPTER THIRTEEN

MONDAY, APRIL 23ᴿᴰ 1985

•••••••

"**E**dwin, it's you mother. How are you?"

"Fine, Mum, never better. You're phoning early." It was 8 a.m. Oakville time.

"Edwin," Mrs. Crowe spoke quickly and excitedly, "you should have told me when you were here a few weeks ago. I spent the weekend at Stonebridge Manor. Carolyn just dropped me off as she is heading back to Paris. It was wonderful." She was gushing with enthusiasm, having difficulty keeping up with her need to explain. "What a beautiful home, and such wonderful people. Oh, it was wonderful!" Ed tried to interrupt, but was not fast enough. "And Carolyn, Edwin—what a lovely young lady. She was so good to me. On the way to the manor—they call it the manor, you see—well she stopped and helped me buy this lovely dress from you. Thank you so much, but it was so expensive— eighty pounds—you shouldn't have, but thank you anyway." Ed's eyes widened. He'd only given Carolyn thirty pounds.

"You welcome, Mum. I'm glad you like it, I . . ." He was interrupted.

"Did you know Carolyn went to Oxford? Of course you do. She is very clever, speaks five languages. Oh, she is so nice. And Penny, that's Lady Stonebridge—what a lovely person. So down to earth and middle-class. Did you know she was born in Neasden? Yes, of course you do, you told me that didn't you? She was so nice to me, and she did say that she liked you, liked your honesty. I'm not sure what she meant, but I agreed with her of course. And the food! Oh, Edwin, the food! And you had me serving Carolyn spaghetti and toad-in-the-hole—what did she think of me I'm sure? And Lord Stonebridge, what a gentleman! He explained the family history, all the way back to the middle-ages. He was so, so . . ."

"English?" Ed offered.

"Yes, that's right—so English! And his job! Well I can't tell you that over the phone can I? Secret information," she whispered. "But oh, what a wonderful weekend! And did you know, Edwin that they go to Ascot—Royal Ascot! And you'll never guess what? When they drive down to Ascot in June, Penny—that's Lady Stonebridge—and Carolyn are going to drop by and I'm going to have my photo taken with them— hats and all! Oh, I am so excited! The neighbours will never believe me. I'm going to tell them of course. They'll be so thrilled. Well maybe not old Mrs. McCann the Irish lady, but I won't let her bother me. This is England isn't it?" She paused, and spoke slowly. "But you should have told me, Edwin. I was quite surprised."

"Yes I should have, Mum," Ed said, smiling, "but I was afraid you wouldn't go."

"Well perhaps you're right," she answered thoughtfully. "But I have to tell the neighbours, so I have to go now." As almost a second thought, she continued. "And how are you, Edwin?"

"I'm fine, Mum. I'm really glad you had a nice time."

"Carolyn is a lovely young lady, Edwin. That's all I have to say."

"Yes she is, Mum. By the way, how's Mrs. Poplowski?"

"The Polish lady? She's fine. Got a new lodger. Nice young man. What makes you ask?"

"Just wondering how the neighbourhood is doing."

They said goodbye and hung up.

Knowing it was late afternoon in Paris; he dialed Carolyn's home number and left a message:

"Oh, to be in England, now that April's there." He paused. "That's all I remember. My mother thinks you walk on water, Carolyn, and I love you so much."

He hung up, and got ready for work.

When he returned home that evening, there was a message on his phone. He pressed the button and closed his eyes. He knew it was Carolyn.

"And whoever wakes in England sees, some morning, unaware, that the lowest boughs and the brushwood sheaf round the elm-tree bole are in tiny leaf. While the chaffinch sings on the orchard bough. In England—now!" There was a pause. "I love you, Ed. Always will."

He grinned and started on supper.

CHAPTER FOURTEEN

SATURDAY MAY 4THTH 1985

•••••••

"Wanna go for a drive?" Pat asked before Ed could speak to answer the phone call.

"Sure, where to?"

"Milton Hilton."

Ed shook his head. "Sorry?"

"That's the name for the jail in Milton. Not far from you. That's where our Mr. DiCosimo is being held; at the Queen's pleasure as you Brits call it."

"How do I get there?"

"You walk down to the lobby and I'm there."

"Now?"

"Now. I knew you'd never say no to a drive with me. My charming personality is more than you can say 'no' to."

"Thirty seconds." He hung up and grabbed his spring jacket.

"So he's agreed to speak with you?" Ed asked as Pat drove along Dundas Street heading to Milton.

"Not quite. He's agreed to speak to someone who may be in a position to recommend a reduction in time to be served if, and only if, he tells us something we deem as useful."

Ed laughed. "So he doesn't know it's 'the cleaning lady' that almost broke his balls that wants to speak to him? You're being pretty cheeky about this if you ask me."

She slowed to turn north on Bronte, then sped up as they entered the gently rolling farm land between Oakville and Milton. "I figured it's worth a try. And if he wants to get mad at me, so be it. But one or both of us need to be there since we know things about the entire matter that can't be passed on to the police."

"Like we're helping MI6 in their enquiries?"

"Exactly."

"And if he tells you to bugger off?"

"Then we bugger off, as you put it, and go for a coffee and donut at Tim Hortons. Life could be a lot worse than that."

Ed sat back in his seat. "Coffee and donuts with my good friend Pat is one of the significant pleasures in my life."

She turned and gave him a dirty look.

"Hey, I mean it," he said quickly. "Maybe see a robin or two. Heck it is spring and hopefully no more snow."

"Obviously you're easy to please today," she commented, putting her foot gently on the brake pedal as they entered the outskirts of Milton.

Pat turned to Ed as she parked the car. "Just go along with what I say, okay?"

"As I always do, Pat, as I always do."

Pat flashed her credentials and they were escorted through the main gate. The security check was quick and complete including a pat-down.

"Did they name that after you?" Ed asked as they were escorted to the secure meeting room. Pat didn't give him the pleasure of a response.

The prison guard opened the steel door with two keys and joined them in the room. Jack DiCosimo sat at a table in the centre of the room with both hands handcuffed to the table. He kept his eyes on his hands in a message of indifference. Two chairs were placed across the table from him. The guard stood by the closed door. "Fifteen minutes," he said coldly.

Pat showed him her credentials. "You can leave us please."

Reluctantly the guard left the room. "Fifteen minutes," he repeated.

Ed and Pat sat. "Nice to see you again," Pat said. "Nice place you have here."

DiCosimo looked up, taking a second to recognise her. "You, you miserable bitch! I ain't speaking to you for nothing."

Pat crossed her arms. "Come on now, Jackie, if it wasn't for me and my friend here you'd be in the big house and not in this nice jail. We did you the favour of having you sent here which is set aside for much nicer ass-holes than the likes of you. I suspect you know this place is for two year sentences or less. You owe us, Jackie."

"Fuck off."

"Okay let's go," Ed said standing.

"What do you say, Jackie?" Pat continued. "You want us to leave or do you want to see if we can reduce your stay by a month or two?"

"Whadda you want?" he grunted. "I told the cops everything to get the deal. I didn't hurt her, didn't touch her. What's the big deal?" He leaned directly into Pat's face. "And don't call me Jackie, okay?"

Pat nodded. "Sure, Jack; or would you prefer I call you Mr. DiCosimo?"

"Just fuck off, okay?"

Ed stood again to leave, but Pat motioned him to sit.

"What we have here is a failure to communicate," Pat said slowly.

DiCosimo looked up grinning. "Yeah! Cool Hand Luke. Great movie. I liked that one big time." He shuffled in his chair. "So what's up? How can I earn a 'get out of jail free' card?" He laughed aloud.

Pat pointed at Ed. "This man here has all the power to get you something. I'm just the middle man."

"You ain't no man, lady." DiCosimo said, almost respectfully.

Ed moved his chair closer to the table. "What we need to know is what the two men told you. We've read your report to the police but I want you to think back and tell me in more detail what they said to you."

"Sure. But keep in mind these guys were Irish. I mean just understanding them wasn't easy. Shit, I didn't know people actually talked like that. Thought it was just on TV, like."

Ed understood. "Okay, so think what they said about the phone call to you. What exactly did they say?"

He closed his eyes to think. "So they were going to phone me when they got to Boston, a shit-hole of an airport according to them."

Ed's senses picked up. "Slowly now. Try to remember exactly what they said."

117

DiCosimo took a deep breath. "Okay the first one says he's going to phone me from Boston, and then the shorter one laughs and says something like, 'then to a shit-hole airport.'" DiCosimo shrugged. "Sorry, that's the best I can do."

As he spoke the guard rapped on the door with a set of keys. "Time!" he shouted.

Ed and Pat stood and walked to the door.

"Well?" DiCosimo asked.

"Maybe," Ed said. "Let me work on it."

"Thanks. And, lady, I think you're okay. Maybe when I get out . . . ?"

"When you get out, Jack, I'll make sure you're looked after for the couple of months by the appropriate authorities, okay? Just keep your nose clean . . . and watch out for those cleaning ladies."

They heard him laugh as the guard closed the door behind them.

Pat turned to Ed. "Maybe? Maybe what for Christ's sake? He said screw all."

Ed tapped the side of his nose and winked. "Maybe, maybe not. Let's get to my place and perhaps I'll make your day."

"Listen, if you're thinking dirty here . . ."

Ed shook his head. "Strictly business, young lady, strictly business."

Pat drove home keeping to the speed limits, admitting that she never exceeded the limits—in anything! Ed didn't push the matter. That was a discussion for another time, he thought.

Ed insisted on a pot of tea before he offered his thoughts to Pat, who, once again, reminded him that a pot of tea was not the solution to resolve the world's problems. Notwithstanding her comments she drank and enjoyed the tea as Ed explained his thinking. He waited for her response.

Pat put her hand to her chin closed her eyes and went into deep thought. She opened her eyes with a smile and reached across the table. "Put it there," she said, gripping his hand, "I think you've got it right on Edwin William; right on!" She rubbed her hands together. "Your phone's secure right?" she asked, knowing that it was. She didn't wait for a reply. "Okay, phone Lord Stonebridge's office—right now."

"It's only just gone seven in the morning," Ed said.

"So what's your point? This ain't chicken shit we're dealing with. Dial the number."

"Okay, but you do the talking. I think it'll come better from you. Perhaps we should get Mr. Cooper involved?"

Pat nodded as the call went through. The phone at the other end rang five times.

"Secure," Lord Stonebridge said flatly.

"Good morning, Lord Stonebridge, it's Pat Weston phoning from Canada. I'm phoning from Mr. Crowe's secure line, and he's on the speaker phone.

There was a short deadly silence. "What's your favourite city, Mr. Crowe?" he asked.

Ed had to think quickly. "Paris in the spring," he answered.

"Proceed, Miss Weston, it's a pleasure to speak with you."

"Thank you, sir. Could we get the General on the line? I think what we have to say may make more sense to him."

Lord Stonebridge nodded. "He's not an early riser, but give me a minute and I'll have him added."

There was a three minute delay which gave Ed time to top them up and rush back to the kitchen table.

"This better be good, Eddie my boy," Mr. Cooper said groggily. "I haven't had my morning coffee yet."

"What we have to say may wake you up," Ed answered.

Lord Stonebridge leaned into his speaker phone. "Before you proceed, Miss Weston, perhaps I should clarify where we're at as it relates to the IRA." It wasn't a question, and he continued without waiting for a response. "Since the beginning of this year 20 members of the army, police, and general public have been killed by the IRA, and more than 50 have been injured. A police officer was shot and killed yesterday. Many of those were shot in the head at point blank range. One soldier was shot 31 times. Two of that soldier's brothers were also in the British army and were both killed by the IRA in 1981. Magee is the IRA's expert in bombing." He spoke without notes. "Am I making myself clear? We want Magee and we want him soon."

Pat sat back from the phone, not sure what to say. Ed motioned her to be calm, and leaned into the speaker. "We think what Miss Weston has to say will be of use, sir."

"Take your time, Miss Weston," Mr. Cooper said calmly. "These are difficult times."

Pat took a deep breathe. "Gentlemen, a bit of background first please. As you know we have the second man in custody, being held under the War Measures Act. He has been interviewed many times by members of the RCMP, CSIS, and the OPP. We have used our best and brightest interviewers. He will not speak, period, except to say he wants to kill the bitch that murdered his brother. That's me, of course, but that's beside the point. The fact is he will not give us any information no matter what we offer in the way of release or getting him home. As a matter of fact, he's recently started on a hunger strike."

"Not good," Lord Stonebridge commented.

"Not good at all, sir, especially for him," Pat replied, "but that is not what we phoned to tell you. Because we're getting nothing from him, we decided to go back to the man our prisoner and his brother hired to hold Ed's boss as possible ransom."

Mr. Cooper was now awake. "I thought he had spilled his guts to get a deal?"

"And so he had," Ed replied, "but Pat, er, Miss Weston, had this idea we should give him one more try; directly with the 'cleaning lady' that laid him out."

Pat rolled her eyes. "We only had fifteen minutes with our Mr. DiCosimo, but Ed's convinced me it was well worth it."

"We're all ears, Miss Weston," Lord Stonebridge said.

"The crux of the matter," Pat continued, "is where the two of them, along with Ed, were heading. Now we know Boston, that was a done deal, but then where, that was the question. The answer was, and I quote here, 'then a shit-hole airport.'" She stopped talking.

"Amsterdam bloody airport!" Mr. Cooper shouted down the line. "Amsterdam; one-hundred percent!' He took a breath. "The name, of course, is Schiphol airport, S-C-H-I-P-O-H-L. We've got them now Lord Stonebridge. No more thinking they're in Amsterdam, they *are* there."

"No doubt in my mind, General, no doubt in my mind," Lord Stonebridge replied enthusiastically. "Well done, Miss Weston and Mr. Crowe. More than a good morning's work." He paused for a moment. "Now I think we can assume that both Mr. Crowe and Miss Andrews were on their way to Amsterdam, no doubt to be held for some kind of ransom. An assumption, of course, but one we will accept as fact, at least for now. Don't give up your day job, Mr. Crowe," he said, as light-hearted as he could muster. "Now, Miss Weston?"

"Yes, sir." Pat almost stood to attention, bur remained seated.

"Miss Weston, a job well done! Now I'm going to get plans in place to transfer all but a few of our staff to Amsterdam in order to double the manpower for the search there. I would like a report faxed to me by Monday morning from your superiors detailing what you told us today. Understood?"

Pat stood to speak. "Yes, sir, and thank you, sir."

After a few minutes of idle chatter about the weather, the call ended.

Ed shook his head. "Well that made things pretty clear, didn't it? I've never heard him speak so bluntly before."

Pat headed for the door. "I gotta go."

Ed helped her on with her coat. "Brilliant work, Pat."

She turned and kissed him quickly. "You got it right, mister, but my getting that report to the manor by Monday morning will make it clear where the information came from." She kissed him quickly again. "Thanks, Ed. For a male bloke you're pretty clever."

She left in a hurry.

"She didn't even finish her tea," Ed said to himself.

CHAPTER FIFTEEN

SATURDAY MAY 18TH, 1985

• • • • • • •

T he phone rang at exactly 7:30 a.m. Ed grabbed the phone, covering his eyes from the sun that was already creeping in his bedroom window.

"Crowe's Nest" he answered as awake as he could.

"Happy Victoria Day weekend," Pat almost shouted into the phone.

"I was just thinking about you," Ed replied, sitting up in bed.

"Bull shit. I just woke you up!"

"Then I must have been dreaming about you."

"Bull, you're full of bull."

He was happy to hear her voice, insults and all. "Okay, let me be more precise. I was thinking about you last night while I was having a beer at the Queen's Head."

"Maybe."

"No maybe. It was a year ago this weekend we met. I distinctly remember you telling me that I was ruining your long weekend."

He could almost hear her smile. "Yeah. You're right. That's why I phoned."

"Sort of happy anniversary?"

"Sort of—you're not ruining my long weekend this year."

"You're at your parent's cottage?"

"Correct the first time. They're out swimming. They must be crazy. The ice has barely left the lake. Age does that I suppose."

"Let's hope we live long enough to find out."

"There you go, cheering me up again."

Pat sounded so much better than before. He was very happy to hear that, but knew better than to raise the issue.

"So are you going to invite me up to meet your parents?"

"Not in a million years."

"Aha! Really good friends then are we?"

She chuckled. "It's not that. It's just that I'm not going to introduce you to my parents when my mother knows you're my lover—if I can use that word."

"That's a good word."

"She'd be beside herself. She wouldn't know what to say, where to have you sleep. She'd never relax. Another time, okay?"

"Of course. I was being pushy. I'd like to see you that's all." There was a long silence. Ed continued. "Did I say something wrong, Pat?"

"No, Ed," Pat said quietly, "you didn't. You said something very nice."

"Another time perhaps?"

"Actually I do need to see you—privately that is."

She had his attention. "Business then?"

"Mostly."

"Name the time and place."

"Your place, Monday morning. Nine o'clock?"

He thought for a moment. "My place, anytime tomorrow?" She didn't respond. "I'll make up the spare bedroom," he added.

"I'll use it!"

"It'll be your exclusive spot."

"Quick thinking, Ed."

"I'll cook us a special supper, one befitting our special friendship *and* our anniversary."

"You are full of it, y'know?"

"Tomorrow then. I'm looking forward to it."

"So am I. Tomorrow it is. Gotta go. My crazy parents are running back from the lake!"

CHAPTER SIXTEEN

SUNDAY MAY 19TH, 1985

• • • • • • •

A t 11 a.m. Ed put away the vacuum. He had awakened early to get ready for Pat's visit. He wanted very much to make it special for her. She had sounded so much better yesterday than when he had seen her just six weeks earlier and even chippier than just two weeks when they had relayed the Amsterdam information to Lord Stonebridge. He wanted desperately to build on her more relaxed manner. The music was ready to go with plenty of Gordon Lightfoot. He had a special tape of Queen, but kept it to one side. His shopping was completed the day before. He had a variety of wines, mostly reds. The guest room was nicely laid out. He was ready.

Pat stopped in a music store in Milton on the way to Oakville. She was not yet ready to shop in downtown Oakville. She was officially 'dead' to some people she might meet. It was too risky. She put her new tape in her purse, smiling to herself as she did. He's not the only clever one, she grinned.

Ed was waiting in the lobby when Pat arrived. He kissed her forehead and took her bag.

"How long have you been waiting here for me?" she asked as they entered the elevator.

"Twenty minutes."

"Am I that predictable?"

"Nope. I just wanted to be here when you arrived. I was planning on sitting there 'til you arrived."

She looked at him suspiciously, but he seemed to mean it. He was dressed in a T-shirt, shorts, and open-toed sandals. No English-style socks. She thought he looked quite Canadian—a lot different than his visit a year earlier when he'd wore long pants, long sleeve shirt and heavy leather shoes. Quite the change she realized. And all for the good.

He showed her to her room, careful not to enter it with her.

"I'll put . . . ," he started.

"The kettle on," she interrupted.

". . . on the kettle," he finished.

Ten minutes later they were sitting on the balcony over-looking Sixteen-Mile Creek as it entered Lake Ontario. A small table between them held their cups of tea and some cheese and biscuits. Ed wanted to reach over and hold Pat's hand but decided not to. Sailing ships were moving out of the Creek and into the Lake. The instructions from the crews could be heard which added to the flavour of the view. Through the screen door the music of Gordon Lightfoot set the stage for a truly Canadian afternoon.

"I have two messages, Ed," Pat announced, finally breaking the silence. "The first one is personal and this is the perfect time and location."

"Do I need to put something stronger in my tea?"

"You tell me after I deliver the message." She turned her chair to face him. "It's about us, you and me. Actually it's more about you. I'm a little nervous to say this, but I feel I must."

Ed turned his chair to face her. He took a deep breath. "I'm listening."

"You have lots of strengths, Ed. You're honest, clever, witty sometimes, and a really, really good friend to have."

He knew the worst was now at hand, and swallowed to make ready.

"Your biggest problem, Ed, is that you're a male. Alpha male and all that, ready to do the right thing, shoot people and even kick them in their privates."

His mouth opened to speak, but he closed it quickly when he could see Pat was not to be interrupted.

"Now when it comes to being honest with me, you fall short." She licked her dry lips. "Now this is where I get a little nervous." She refocused on his now confused look. "I think you love me, Ed. Not love me like you want to marry me, but love me like we're super great friends. We like being in each other's company. We like it when we make love, and we're good at it. I want you to tell me that you love me, Ed, especially when we make love. But you won't because you think I'll expect a real engagement ring, a wedding and everything that goes with it. I don't. I love you, but not like that—it's that simple. I just want you to be honest with me. Is that asking too much, Ed?'

He blinked several times, trying to absorb everything he had just heard. He shook his head. "No, that's not asking too much, Pat," he stuttered. "Can you give me time to get my head in gear?"

"Two minutes. I'll go top up our tea." She picked up their cups and went into the apartment. She gave him three minutes then re-joined him on the balcony. Putting the two cups down, she looked at him eye to eye.

He gulped, struggling to respond without losing a good friend and hurting her feelings. "Can I say, Pat, that yes I do love you in the way you described, and can I try to define it as love with a small 'L'? I know it's not a perfect description, but it's the best I could come up with while being honest at the same time."

Pat picked up her cup of tea without taking her eyes of Ed. "Love with a small 'L' you say?" She sipped her tea. She put her cup down with a jolt. "Perfect! Just what I intended. See, you do have it in you to envision things in a female fashion. Well done." She smiled genuinely. "Okay, that's over with!"

Ed took her hands and kissed them both. "I love you, Pat," he said, "and we don't have to be making love for me to admit it."

"Good," she said, looking around. "Because if we tried it out here, we'd fall to our deaths!"

They turned back to the lake, picked up their cups of teas and held hands across the table.

"Nice day," Ed commented.

"Wonderful day," Pat smiled.

They drank more tea than Pat thought possible. Little was spoken between them as they watched the early-in-the-season sailors head out into Lake Ontario.

She squeezed his hand, and turned to him. "So what do you want to do?"

"We could go in and do a bit of snogging."

"Snogging? What the heck's snogging?"

He turned to her. "Kissing. It's a bit of British slang."

She pulled a face. "Yuck! What a horrible word for kissing. I think *necking* sounds a bit more romantic than snogging!"

"Okay. I buy that. Let me finish reading your palm from a couple of weeks ago."

She held out her left hand, which he took and studied. "I see your love-line is longer than it was a few weeks ago."

She smiled. "I think it's longer than it was last night. I felt it grow just a tad when you told me you loved me. It felt good."

He continued studying her palm, gently following her lines with his finger. She giggled as he tickled her.

"Ah, ha!" he said, looking closer. "I see something interesting."

She sat up and moved closer. "What do you see, Oh great one?"

"I see a man. A man who wants to neck with you."

"Oh my!" she wailed quietly. "Whatever should I do?"

"Be careful. This man has intentions. He wants to kiss you. He wants to start by kissing your forehead, then your neck, and then—well, I'm embarrassed to say where next!" Ed sat back and let her hand slip from his.

She shoved her hand back at him. "Tell me," she demanded demurely. "Where does he want to kiss me next?"

Leaning forward he whispered in her ear. "He wants to kiss your lovely breasts. He wants to lick them and then suck gently on your beautiful nipples."

Pat stood up and brushed away at her hands as if to remove the story. "Well he's not going to is he? Who does he think he is? What kind of a woman does he think I am?" She reached down and took his two hands in hers. "You, on the other hand, are going to do just that. And a lot more besides." She pulled him up from the chair, turned him to face the apartment, and pushed him gently. "And when we get inside, I'm going to tell you what I'm going to do to you!"

They quickly entered the apartment. They wrapped their arms around each other and held tight. Pat pushed him away far enough to lift off his T-shirt. Looking up and smiling she proceeded to kiss his chest and suck on his nipples. Dropping to her knees, she quickly removed his shorts and underwear. Holding his now swollen cock, she kissed it lovingly and then allowed him to put it fully in her mouth.

Gasping with pleasure he pulled her up as fast as he could and undressed her—kissing and licking her as he did. Without speaking he took her hand and walked her to his bedroom.

He closed the curtains as she pulled back the covers and lay on the bed. "I want you in me now, Ed. Right now."

He joined her on the bed, spread her legs and entered her moist warm body. He thrust himself into her, forcing her to arch up and take him all. "I love you, Pat." He thrust again and again and again. He slowed down, keeping his cock in her. "Open your eyes, Pat," he asked.

She opened her eyes, loving the feeling of his body—wanting it to never stop.

He reached down and held a breast in each hand. "I love you," he smiled, pinching each nipple between his fingers. "Now close your eyes and let me make you come."

She mouthed 'I love you', closing her eyes to enjoy the pleasure that he was about to offer her. She moved with his thrusts, lost in the warmth of their loving.

Pat woke up; Ed's face was just inches from hers.

"You fell asleep," he laughed.

"After," she murmured, "not during."

He kissed her and licked her lips. "Thank you. That was wonderful."

"Thank you for loving me, Ed. It means a great deal to me." She snuggled into him. "You're my favourite lover," she whispered. "My only lover perhaps, but my favourite anyway."

He reached over and gently smacked her bum. "Let's go," he said. "I have supper to make."

They both jumped out of bed and raced to gather their clothes to get dressed. Pat won handily, hiding her bra under the sofa.

Ed was in the kitchen area cutting and dicing supper. Pat had opened a bottle of wine and was letting it breathe.

Pat wandered over to watch him cook. "Before we start drinking we need to chat," she said in a business-like fashion.

"Okay. You're the one with the up-date. You talk, I'll listen."

She pulled a face. "Well the bad news is we may not be going cruising in June."

Ed looked up, disappointment obvious in his face. "I hope it's because you have some good news."

She shrugged and tilted her head. "Maybe, maybe not. Our man, Patrick Magee that is, as we know, definitely in Amsterdam, Holland."

"The Netherlands," Ed corrected.

She narrowed her eyes to show disapproval. "Okay one of the two Provinces of the Netherlands, namely North Holland or South Holland."

Ed looked down to hide his face. "Sorry 'bout that."

She continued. "So the plan, Operation Tea Party that is, is to find him and go get him, no matter where he is. For lack of a better word, we kidnap him. We get him back to the U.K. where's he'll be arrested for the Brighton Bombing affair."

"We?"

"You and me."

He put the knife down and picked up a towel to wipe his hands. "Just you and me? Christ, could they pick anyone less capable for the job? Last time I tried this, the man killed himself."

Pats face went white. "And you think if this one doesn't kill himself, then I'll kill the son-of-a-bitch? Is that what you think?"

Ed walked around the kitchen island and took her hands. "No. That's not what I said, and that's not what I meant." He sat at the table, motioning her to do the same. Reluctantly she sat. He raised his hand to calm the conversation. "What I meant was . . . what I was trying to say was . . . Shit, I don't know what I was trying to say. You caught me off guard, that's all. I'm sorry if I sounded rude. Forgive me?"

"No."

"Please?"

"No."

"Pretty please with bells on?"

"Maybe." She lifted her head and took a deep breath. "Okay, you're forgiven," she smiled. The smile faded. "But don't you dare question me in that fashion again. Do you think we planned this on the back of an envelope?"

Ed stood up. "Let's go back to where we were." He walked into the kitchen area, and Pat stayed on her side of the island. "So what's the plan?" he asked.

Pat waited to respond to gain some ground. "There will be four of us. You and me, Carolyn, and a lady I don't know. Sue Banks."

"I've met Sue," Ed said excitedly. "She was part of Operation Hawfinch. She's Canadian. Lives in Ottawa. I didn't know she was with MI6."

"Well, if we published a book on everything you don't know . . ." She left it at that.

"Keep going," he muttered.

"The official party is you and me. The others are back-up. They're MI6, we're not."

He nodded, understanding the need to not have it appear that Magee was brought to Britain against his will by the British authorities.

"Got it."

"We get him back to Britain and we head back as fast as a flash to Canada. They arrest him, the police not MI6, and no-ones the wiser."

Ed nodded. "And your father's brother's name is Robert!"

"What!"

"Bob's your uncle."

"As you wish." She rolled her eyes in irritation, but inwardly told herself to remember that one!

Ed thought about the plan. "And what about the man you still have in custody?"

"First, his name is Griffin—Daniel David Griffin. Goes by Dee Dee. The dead man was his brother Tony." Pat spoke without any visual concern of talking about the man she had killed. "Mr. Griffin will be released and returned to Ireland: or more correctly Eire if you're going to be precise about everything."

"And you'll let him go shortly after Magee is back in Britain and arrested?"

"You've got it!"

"Where it may look to some that he had a part in the catching of Magee?"

She smiled broadly. "Right on, mister. Right on!"

"You are a sneaky lady, I must say."

"You know what?" Pat said, now getting excited. "That SOB still refers to me as 'the Bitch!'. Me, a bitch! Hell if it weren't for me he'd be pushing up daisies. Miserable SOB should be thanking me."

"I see you have a point of view on this then?" Ed asked looking up from his cooking.

She calmed down. "Anyway, that's the plan. Every MI6 agent in Europe is in Amsterdam working on finding him. It's just a matter of time—and money. *Friends* will do lots of un-friendly things for money."

"Much?"

"Lots."

"Good."

"So the cruise has to be cancelled. Just in case something breaks."

Ed looked up. "You mean postponed?"

She winked. "I meant postponed. Perhaps in the fall."

"That's autumn is it?"

"Yes it is. And this is North America."

Ed walked around the island, taking off his apron. "Yes it is. And this is the Victoria Day Weekend—our anniversary. Gimme a kiss!"

She stood on her toes to kiss him. "I'll pour the wine."

"About bloody time, I'd say. Cooking can make you thirsty."

"So can sex," Pat added.

"Yes," Ed agreed. "Wonderful sex with a person you love."

"Shush up, Ed. You'll have me in tears."

While Ed continued cooking, Pat looked for some music. She flipped around the tapes. Lots of Gordon Lightfoot. She appreciated that. She saw a tape at the back and picked it up. She turned to Ed with a cold look. "What's this?"

Ed looked up, now realizing his mistake. "I can't see it from here."

Pat walked over to him with the tape held out in front of her.

"Ah, that's Queen," Ed grinned shyly. "I like them."

"Really? I'm surprised. Rather heavy for you I'd have thought."

"Got to mix it up a bit, eh?"

She looked at the tape and then at Ed. He could see she was not amused. "Do you know the second song?" she asked.

He thought for a moment. He shook his head. "Not sure exactly."

Her eyes opened wide in feign surprise. "Try thinking and not lying."

He put down the food and knife in his hand. "Okay, it's Bohemian Rhapsody."

"Yes it is. And do you know the words to the second verse in the song?"

He looked to the ceiling for help. Nothing materialized. "Sort of."

"So *sort of* tell me the words. Please."

He licked his lips, closed his eyes and spoke quietly. "*Mama, just killed a man . . .*" Opening his eyes he shrugged in regret.

"Please continue."

"*Put a gun against his head, . .*" She waved him on. He continued, speaking so softly she could barely hear him. "*Pulled the trigger, now he's dead.*"

She put the tape down. "Very good. So let me see if I can get the picture clear here. You wanted to suggest that somehow my hearing that song would make me feel better? Or better yet, perhaps you thought I should play the song for my mother? The old *wink, wink* message perhaps? Your basic Psychology 1-0-1. And this from a bloke that never ever took a Psychology course. Is that it, Mr. Crowe? Here to save my sanity are you?"

He felt their friendship slipping away with every question she asked. He could not allow that to happen, but he was stuck for words. His head was spinning for answers, but nothing worked. He spread his hands in despair, shaking his head. He was verbally and emotionally lost.

"Now, Mr. Crowe," Pat continued calmly, "if you go to my purse, you'll find a tape I thought would be appropriate for our get together." She pointed to her purse by the front door. "Would you please?"

Ed walked over to the purse. It seemed large enough to hold fifty tapes and still have plenty of room left over. He decided not to raise that point of information. Picking up the purse, he dug around until he found the tape. He looked at it and span around to Pat.

"You little bugger," he shouted, holding up a Queen tape. "You rotten little bugger. It's the same bloody tape." He didn't know if he wanted to laugh or cry. "I'll get you for this, Miss Weston. You almost had me in tears there. You little . . ."

Pat's face was calm. "I'd appreciate your not adding the adjective 'little' to every name you're going to call me. It offends my personal human rights as a height-challenged female minority. I have feelings too, you know."

He walked over to her and stooped down to meet her face to face, only inches apart. "Okay you big shit-head, I'm never going to make love to you again."

She kept her straight face. "Really?"

"Really."

"Do you know," she grinned, trying not to laugh, "that I don't have a bra on, and being this close to you is making my nipples go hard?"

He pulled her into him and held her tight, laughing out loud. "You're a wonderful person," he said, kissing the top of her head.

She clung to him. "What else?"

"You have a great sense of humour."

"What else?"

He held her away and looked down at her. "I love you."

"Okay," she smiled, pushing him toward the kitchen. "Supper!"

"Hey, what about those lovely hard nipples of yours?"

"I lied. You're not that sexy."

"Maybe," he commented, walking into the kitchen area, "but I am a good cook."

"We'll see. I'll top up our wine."

With the meal finished and the dishes in the dishwasher, they headed back onto the balcony with their wine. The sun was slowly disappearing and soon early fireworks would begin. Hardy sailors were moving out of the creek into Lake Ontario to watch the Sunday night display. The bigger shows would be the next night.

Pat took a sip of her wine. "So you deserve an up-date, I suppose?"

"Well we are lovers."

"Yes," she smiled sweetly, "we are." She put her wine glass down, and turned to face him. "When I was here at the end of March you helped me see that pulling the trigger on Mr Griffin was the right thing to do. In killing him, I saved lives . . ."

133

"Including ours," Ed added quickly.

"Including ours, yes. Now it wasn't a quick over-night forget-about-killing-a-man situation. I'd not slept well before we chatted. But my sleeping got better and the more I slept through the night the easier it was for me to accept the fact that I did the right thing. But, Ed," she reached over and rested her hand on his arm, "it wasn't easy. I don't want to go through that again—ever."

He picked up her hand and kissed it. "All the more reason we need to be very careful when, or if, Operation Tea Party requires our involvement."

"There is no 'if', Ed, only 'when'. You don't try blowing up the British Cabinet and get away with it. Ask Guy Fawkes, right?"

He took a sip of his wine and nodded. He smiled as they turned to watch the first fireworks explode below them. He was worried about their future role, but tonight wasn't the time to discuss his concerns. It was a night to celebrate the un-official start to Canada's summer season.

CHAPTER SEVENTEEN

MONDAY, MAY 20TH 1985

• • • • • • •

P at crept silently into Ed's bedroom. She was fully dressed. Her bag was by the door to the hallway. It was 6:30 am. Blowing him a kiss she left his room, picked up her bag and left the apartment.

Ed heard the door close, waited for thirty seconds, got out of bed and walked into the living room area. As he had expected there was a note for him. It was on the kitchen table. He unfolded it, and read Pat's note.

Dear Ed

I love you very much. More than I can verbalize—it's just not my skill set.

I want to go back via my parent's place. I know if I woke you up, I'd lose two wonderful hours in your arms. I'll miss that. Thank you for loving me and for a great time. You're a very special person.

This isn't a Dear John letter, not even close. I'll keep in touch.

Love, Pat

He folded the note and put it in a kitchen drawer. Pat was so much better than she had been in March, which was clearly obvious—even to a bloke that had never taken a course in Psychology. He decided he would send her more flowers later that week to her office address. She'd like that. He put the kettle on for the mandatory morning cup of tea.

CHAPTER EIGHTEEN

SATURDAY JUNE 22ND, 1985.

• • • • • • •

E d entered his apartment and quickly ran to pick up the phone that
was ringing.
"Crowe's Nest," he said clearly.
"Hi. Whatcha doing?" Pat asked.
"Just got back from doing some bird watching. Long time, no see."
"Yeah, a month. I've been meaning to phone. Been busy."
Ed fully understood. "Personal or business?"
"Business. You alone?"
He chuckled. "Oh yeah. Fire away."
"Very funny," she laughed. "Nice play on words."
"Unintended this time."
Her voice changed. "Can you be ready to leave in an hour?"
He thought through his week ahead. "I'm okay; just have to let
Diane know."
"Done! We had a quick chat. She likes the way you work."
"Thanks. How long we going for?"
"A week maybe."
"Do I need bring anything?"
"What would your mother recommend?"
"Lots of underwear."
"Then that's it. Plus your passport of course."
"Then I'll be ready in an hour. You're picking me up?"

"No. I'll see you at Toronto Island Airport. About two hours then?"

He looked at his watch. "Seven p.m. it is. Looking forward to seeing you."

"We'll catch up on the plane." She paused. "My first international flight. Looking forward to it."

"Hey, listen," Ed said quietly, "you've heard the news right?"

There was a long silence before Pat replied. "You mean about the Air India flight that went down today?"

"Yeah. I know we're probably on a special flight, but wanted to at least talk about it."

"I hear ya," Pat replied thoughtfully. "I guess we have to keep calm and carry on."

"Yes. Yes we do. End of that discussion then?"

"End of discussion. See you soon."

"Bye for now." He hung up, walked to his bedroom and started packing.

"Wow," Pat exclaimed as the jet left the ground and took off at a forty-five degree angle. She had to pull on the seat in front of her to look out of the window. She pointed out the places she could recognize until they were well over Lake Ontario, with New York State now visible ahead. The plane levelled off, and she sat back to relax.

"Coffee?" Ed asked, motioning to the back of the plane.

"No tea?" she laughed.

"'Fraid not. Why don't you check with the pilot and co-pilot to see if they would like some?"

She carefully made her way to the cockpit, returning two minutes later. "They showed me the plane's equipment. Everything but the kitchen sink."

Ed brewed the coffee, delivered two cups to the cockpit and made his way back to the table at the rear of the plane. Pat sat at the table with a small notebook open.

Ed took a sip of the hot coffee. "Straight to business then?"

Pat looked up from the notebook, smiled, and looking back down closed the book. "Sorry. How are you, Ed?"

"Very well, thanks. How are you? I don't mean to sound personal, but you're looking very perky."

"Nice word," she nodded. "Yes, I'd say I'm feeling perky."

"Great. Glad to hear it." He looked to the notebook. "Let's go then. I've been anticipating your call. Nice to be working together."

"One personal question, Ed. When you got in the plane, you didn't give me a hug. Reason?"

"One doesn't hug one's boss in front of other people." He intended to live up to his agreement, or was it an order, from Carolyn.

Pat nodded her appreciation with a huge smile, then flipped open the notebook to the first page and began reading.

"As we know, our man is in Amsterdam. He's moving from location to location, but we've got him on the run. His resting stops are reducing daily. He knows we've got him, so he's more dangerous than ever. He's got two goons running with him. They're carrying weapons. Not sure of calibre, but small enough to hide while wearing a suit. Number 10 is authorizing all and any expense. They want a result."

"And we fit in where?" Ed asked, getting excited about the idea of action.

"We, that's the big we, are setting up three teams with four members each. We're one team, you, me, Carolyn, and Sue Banks. So the chances of our seeing any real action are one in three of course. The idea is to reduce the stress on setting up just one team."

"Makes sense. Do we know the other teams?"

"No. We won't know the other teams. So if we bump into each other, or if something goes wrong, our identities are protected. What we do know is each team has two Brits on it, and two foreigners—so to speak—different nationalities."

Ed smiled. "Let me guess; one team from the US and one team from Australia?"

Pat shrugged. "What do I know?"

"More than you're telling, but that's fine. And here's another guess. You want to make sure *we* catch our man before the Americans do."

Pat huffed. "That small-town thinking never crossed my mind."

"Never?"

"Well maybe once or twice."

Ed thought back to the time Pat had taken him to Niagara Falls and made sure to point out that the Canadian falls were prettier than the US falls. "Our falls are prettier than their falls," he reminded her.

"Well of course it matters for Christ's sake," Pat snapped, closing her notebook. "If those CIA types get him, we'll never hear the end of it." She calmed down. "I know that sounds silly, but it's just the way it is. I don't want them pulling a World War Two on us: coming in at the last minute and claiming all the credit."

"Yes, boss," Ed saluted. "First one to Berlin, right?"

Pat smiled. "Kind of, yeah. And don't call me boss!"

"Okay, guv'nor."

"That's worse."

"Yes, ma'am."

Pat shook her head. "Just top-up the coffee, okay?"

"Okay, boss," he said standing.

Pat rolled her eyes in defeat. She watched Ed make the coffee. "There is one thing I want to say, Ed. I'm really glad we're working together on this."

Ed didn't turn, but carried on with the coffee. "So am I, Pat. So am I."

When the coffee was poured he re-joined her at the table. "My final question, Pat. Who's the lead on our team, you or Carolyn?"

"Carolyn," Pat replied. "It's their game, we're outside help. Is that okay with you?"

"Absolutely," Ed said. "Just need to know. Don't want to get caught in the middle of two strong-willed bosses."

"I'll tell her you said that," Pat laughed. "I'm sure she'll be right chuffed."

"Chuffed? Working on your English-English are you?"

Pat smiled and sat up straight. "How's this then?" She spoke with an English accent. "I say old chap, is this the way to the W.C? Blimey, I fink it is. Just past the lollypop lady, mate!" Pat smiled, and took a breath. "And; Sharrup will ya. Don't say a dixie bird."

Ed laughed at her accent. "Very good, very good indeed. But what's a dixie bird?"

"Hey, how do I know? *Not a dixie bird*—that's what they said on East Enders."

He chuckled out loud. "I think you'll find they said *not a dickey bird*. Dickey bird rhymes with word, so it means *not a word*."

"Well I was close," Pat said indignantly.

"You were very good, Pat. I'd be proud to introduce you to the Queen."

She sniffed the air. "Sharrup will ya."

"Yes, boss," Ed smiled.

"Listen," Pat said seriously, "there is one thing I want to say personally—and then it's all business. Okay?"

Ed nodded, taking a sip of his coffee.

Pat licked her lips. "You know how we feel about each other, Ed, and I am very proud of our relationship. But as we head into this we must simply look and act professionally. I know I can act like a bit of a pain in the you-know-where sometimes, but that's me at work—not an act. I just want you to understand and appreciate that." She pursed her lips. "Okay?"

"Nothing wrong with being dedicated. I fully understand. Just remember it goes both ways. I'm more inclined to accept things for what they are and I know I can seem too casual at times."

"Really?" Pat said sarcastically. "I hadn't noticed."

"Then we make a good team?"

"Yes we do. Let's go over some of the information I have to go on and then get a few hours of kip in."

"Work and a good kip! Sounds perfect. I'll pour us some more coffee, boss."

"Thanks, Ed. You make being a boss sound like fun!"

They reviewed the photos and backgrounds of the IRA members in Amsterdam, and reviewed in some detail a street map of Amsterdam. Ed was surprised how many canals and bridges there were. It was obviously a well-designed city with a lot of history.

It was difficult for them to fall asleep with so much running through their mind, but eventually exhaustion took over and they each slipped into a fretful, uneasy sleep.

CHAPTER NINETEEN

SUNDAY, JUNE 23RD, 1985

• • • ● ● ● • •

E d woke after only a few hours sleep. He checked with the pilot. They were half an hour from London. They would arrive at 5 a.m. Two passengers would join them, the pilot had told him, and they would immediately fly on to Amsterdam. Estimated time of arrival in Amsterdam 7 a.m. local time. Making sure not to wake Pat, he put on some fresh coffee.

Pat woke as the plane landed. She shook her head, sorting out where she was. Ed sat across the aisle from her holding two cups of steaming-hot coffee.

"Morning, boss. Welcome to England. Here's your coffee. We'll be joined by Carolyn and Sue and immediately flown to Amsterdam. Estimated time of arrival in Amsterdam 7 a.m. local time. Have a nice day."

Pat waved off the coffee. "I've got to freshen up. My make-up is a mess. I'll be back." She picked up her purse and staggered to the washroom as the plane taxied slowly across the airfield.

Ed headed back to pour more cups of coffee.

Pat was feeling respectably refreshed as Carolyn and Sue entered the plane. The pilot wasted no time in formalities, he just headed quickly back to the cockpit. Ten minutes later they were in the air and levelled off.

Carolyn introduced Pat and Sue and the four sat around the board table, coffees in hand. Pat felt particularly friendly toward Sue immediately. It wasn't often she met people shorter than herself. Pat felt she had at least half an inch on Sue.

Sue explained her role, outlining that although she was Canadian, she was currently on loan, full time, with MI6. She and Pat exchanged backgrounds and agreed they would get together next time they were both in Canada.

"Nice to see you made it alive," Sue said, turning to Ed. "Last time I saw you, you were in a body bag looking decidedly dead." All knew she was referring to his trip to HMS Arc Royal from Tripoli, Libya where he had been *officially* shot and killed by Colonel Gaddafi.

"Thanks, Sue. It's nice to see you again."

There was no time for further catching up. Carolyn reached into her carry-on bag and spread a large-scale map of Amsterdam on the table. "Welcome to Operation Tea Party." She spoke calmly. Reaching back into her purse she withdrew a gun and holster and handed them to Ed.

"Fully loaded, Mr. Crowe." She turned to Pat. "I assume . . ?"

"In my purse and fully loaded," Pat confirmed.

"That's my boss." Ed smiled.

Carolyn raised her hand. "Good point, Mr. Crowe. We have to decide what we are going to call each other. Pat, since Ed calls you boss—you're Boss. Let's call Ed—Mister, and if you agree I'll be— Miss. Sue, what would you like to be called?"

Ed spoke up. "I'd suggest—Leader. It fits, and it will add to the confusion."

Sue nodded.

"Then it's agreed," Carolyn stated. "We start using them now and we don't change until we get back on British soil."

The rest agreed with a nod. The quick decision made them feel closer and it brought to mind the seriousness of the situation at hand.

Carolyn flattened out the map and pointed to a central location. "That is Dam Square. That's our location. The Amsterdam police have seen Magee and his bodyguards visit the square from time to time. Since neither Magee nor the others have done anything wrong in Amsterdam the police can do nothing about them. Not that we want them to anyway. They have unofficially agreed to leave us to ourselves but are working with us. The chief of police is especially happy to be working with Canadians. He is old enough to remember how the First Canadian Army liberated his country during the Second World War. What I didn't know until recently was that Princess Margriet was born in Ottawa where her parents were in exile, and the maternity ward of the Ottawa Civic Hospital was declared part of the Netherlands—so in effect she was born on Dutch soil."

"I did not know that," Pat said.

"You do now, Boss," Carolyn smiled. "A bit of trivia to save for a rainy day."

"Does that mean they think we'll likely be the team to see action, Miss?" Sue asked.

"Very much so," Carolyn replied. "I think they want the Canadians to get the credit. But who knows when. If not today maybe tomorrow; or next week perhaps. I've booked four rooms at The Best Western, just up the street from Dam Square. None of the three teams head home until we've got our man."

Pat smiled at the thought of being part of a successful operation where her nationality was an important factor.

Carolyn continued. "The two other teams are located at Amsterdam Airport and the residential area of Amteleen, here on the map. As you can see it is between downtown and the airport. A good location for either a quick get away or to get lost in the busy city streets."

"Which team has the Americans?" Pat asked casually.

Carolyn gave her an enquiring look. "The airport. But this isn't a competition."

"Absolutely not," Pat agreed. "Never crossed my mind," she lied

Carolyn went over the map of downtown in detail, showing which directions Magee and his men had mostly entered Dam Square. "There are seven entrances and the one they have used most is the entrance from the north. This entrance is from a shopping area. The street is narrow and there is an outside café right at the entrance. It allows them a good look-see before they actually enter the square. We'll assume that's where they'll enter from."

"More people, more risk," Sue commented, thinking out loud.

"Absolutely," Carolyn agreed. "So I suggest we separate and mingle. If we're lucky the police will give us advance warning. They have a lot of special officers working on this case. Rest assured if our man comes near the square, we'd know about him. But," she emphasised, "we are on our own. They will help us, but they cannot physically assist us."

"How will we know?" Ed asked.

"I'll have a walkie-talkie and will be in touch with the Amsterdam police. So while keeping your eyes out for our man, you will need to watch and follow my instructions. Any questions?"

The hour flight went quickly. Carolyn answered the questions as best she could while making it clear the takedown, if in fact there was a takedown, would have a life of its own.

"Number one priority is our own safety and the safety of the people of Amsterdam," Carolyn wrapped up as the plane descended into Amsterdam airport, "but if you have to shoot—shoot to kill. We don't want any stray bullets."

"Been there," Pat mumbled.

Ed nodded as he strapped his gun and holster to his left ankle.

Sue opened her purse, making sure her gun was well situated. "Understood," she said.

"Could I ask one more question, Miss?" Ed asked.

"Of course, Mister," Carolyn answered with a sly wink. "What might that be?"

Ed returned the wink with a broad smile. "Do we ever get to eat?"

"Full continental breakfast in the drive downtown." Carolyn replied. "And I've ordered tea as a special treat."

"I like you, Miss," Sue commented. "Tea and crumpets! What better meal before the challenge ahead?"

Laughing and discussing whether it was a boot or a trunk, they put their carry-on luggage in it. The ladies kept their purses with them. It was a full size limousine that allowed plenty of room for four people to relax and enjoy breakfast. The driver gave Carolyn a walkie-talkie, and they all agreed they had not seen one as small. After finishing their meals each of them relaxed and took in the view of Amsterdam. There seemed to be an unending number of bridges across narrow and beautiful canals. The live-in barges that adorned the canals were colourful and well kept.

"The City of Canals," Carolyn said quietly, almost to herself.

"And the City of Anne Frank," Sue reminded them.

Pat turned away from the window, shaking her head. "Well you couldn't get more different than those two scenarios can you?"

"Well not to make comparisons in any way," Carolyn added, "let's hope it will soon be considered the City where the Brighton Bomber was captured."

"By the A team!" Pat said enthusiastically, punching the air.

All four shook hands and felt good about the adventure they were heading into

The limousine pulled into Dam Square and the four team members exited to a busy and magnificent setting. The Royal Palace that faced onto the square was a beautiful four story building with a domed clock tower at its centre. On the left side of the square facing the Palace was the Madam Tussaud building which was equally magnificent and eye-catching. Trams ran around the square picking up and dropping off passengers and people were everywhere. It was a photographer's delight and people were either taking photos or having their photo taken. It was busy, Ed thought, very busy. Turning to face north they quickly recognized the café where their man and his bodyguards usually entered the square.

Carolyn pulled them together, and spoke quietly. "It is a Sunday and it is June. I suppose we shouldn't be too surprised at the volume of people. So let's be extremely careful. Comments?"

Pat sighed as she looked around at the hundreds of people gathered in the square. "For the first time, I'm hoping one of the other teams gets our man." She shrugged. "Preferably not the Yanks of course!"

Her comments relaxed them somewhat and Carolyn pointed out where each one should stand. They had reviewed several recent photos of Magee, and they each felt confident in their ability to identify him.

"I'll remain in the centre of the square," Carolyn reminded them. "So if you see me in the process of taking a photograph, hardly an unusual event around here, then you'll know our man is on his way, and he'll be coming from the direction I'll be facing. If anyone sees him first, then pretend you're taking a photo and I'll follow your direction. We close ranks and then follow our plan. Final questions?"

There were none.

"Then as they say on the television," Carolyn said, looking at each of them, "let's do it."

Sue stayed where they were on the south side of the square. Ed went to west side and Pat to the east. Carolyn walked to the centre. As had been agreed each of them started searching their own area, while keeping Carolyn constantly in sight.

As Ed walked to his designated area he looked at his watch. It was 8:45a.m. Realizing it would only get busier as the day proceeded, he wondered if their plan could succeed. He set the thought aside and walked slowly around smiling and doing his best to blend in. While everyone else was admiring the magnificence of the buildings that created the square, he trained his eyes on the people, but doing so in a way that he didn't make eye contact with any one person for more than a second. Every few seconds he would sweep the entire view of the square, catching Carolyn in his sight as he took in the wider view. She deliberately had her hands low. Her left hand was in her jeans pocket, and she gripped her purse tightly with her right hand as if worried about someone snatching her purse.

The crowds got larger and slowly groups of school-aged children, trying unsuccessfully to be controlled by their parents, were joining the crowds. Ed's heart sank at the thought of guns being fired in such a crowd. He looked to Carolyn for direction, but got none. He continued searching and smiling.

Shortly after 10 a.m. Ed felt that something was happening. The groupings of school children were slowly moving toward him and beyond him to the Palace. Carolyn was now facing south and talking into the walkie-talkie. He scanned for Sue and Pat. Both must have noticed the same shift in surroundings, they too were looking toward Carolyn and appeared more alert. He slowly did a 180-degree turn, and saw what he was expecting as he completed the turn.

Carolyn was now facing north and in the pose of taking a photograph. Against all of his natural instincts to follow her viewing, he didn't. He slowly, almost agonizingly slowly, walked toward Carolyn. He wanted to reach her at the same time as Sue and Pat, both of who were now moving toward the square's centre. He let people cross in front of him, smiling at them as he did. He was the most obvious of kindly tourist, but his heart was beating at such a pace he worried that others could hear it. It wasn't possible, he knew—so he kept smiling until he reached Carolyn. He stood several steps behind her, and within fifteen seconds

Sue and Pat stood with him. All three smiling and nodding to each other like three rag dolls.

Carolyn turned and joined them. She spoke calmly but quickly. "Three minutes. They're coming through the café. As we planned, Mister to the left, me and Leader in the centre, Boss to the right. The police have managed to get the children out of firing line. They should be in the Palace by the time our man arrives. Ready?"

All three nodded.

"Then let's have a Tea Party," Carolyn said.

Talking gibberish to each other they walked slowly northward across the square. The goal was to be as close to the centre of the square as possible—more space, fewer people. It seemed to take forever, but finally Ed saw the three men.

"Got 'em," he said gritting his teeth in a smile. "About thirty seconds."

The ladies adjusted their purses and un-zipped them.

Carolyn stopped to look around, signalling that they would now wait for the men to reach them. Between them and the men there were two Japanese couples taking many photos of themselves and the square. At an excruciatingly slow pace the two Japanese couples re-grouped and walked slowly toward the Royal Palace. The three men were now twelve feet away. Ed bent down to adjust his shoelace. The ladies hands slipped into their purses. The people around them kept talking and carrying on like everything was fine.

Magee sensed something wrong. The four people ahead of them were out of place. They were not tourists. He squinted to narrow his view, but it happened before he could raise his concerns to the bodyguards on either side of him.

Ed stood from a crouched position holding his gun on the man on the left. Carolyn and Sue had their guns trained on Magee's chest, and Pat's gun was aimed at the head of the man on the right.

"Don't think of moving," Carolyn shouted. "Raise you hands above your head and keep them there."

Magee raised his hands as directed, smiling as he did. The men on either side kept their hands low, each looking for an opportunity, their fingers twitching in frustration, their faces red with anger.

Magee recognized Carolyn and grinned. "Well if it isn't my prostitute friend from Paris. Watcha gon'na do young lady?" Magee spoke in his deep Irish accent, looking around the square. "Lots of people here. Wouldn't want to get anyone hurt, would we now?"

While some people moved away slowly from them, many stood and watched, almost mesmerized. The Japanese couples were only twenty feet away and one man raised his camera to take a photo of the scene.

Carolyn made a decision not in the plan. She lowered her gun, moved to her left and shot the man in front of Ed in his left leg. He fell screaming to the ground and all hell broke loose.

People started screaming and running away from them in all directions. The two Japanese couples now turned and ran dropping their camera's in the confusion. Magee gestured to lower his hands, but motions from Carolyn's and Sue's guns stopped him cold. The man on the right swore and was tempted to move, but stopped instantly as Pat lowered her gun to his groin area. "Move and I'll blow your balls into the middle of next week," she shouted. He wanted to cover himself, but stood tall and proud in defiance.

Ed walked to the man in front of him. The man was holding his leg screaming for help.

"Undo your jacket." Ed said calmly.

"Fuck you," the man managed.

Ed smacked him across the face with his gun. The man collapsed unconscious. Ed undid the man's jacket, with two fingers pulled out a gun from his belt and slid it across the ground in front of Carolyn. Without looking down, Carolyn slid the gun behind her with her foot.

Pat kept her gun trained on his groin area. "You're next," she said. "The sooner we get your gun, the sooner your friend gets help. Your choice."

The man looked at Magee but got no direction. "Fuck you all," he grunted. "You can have my gun, but I swear to God I'll get you all later."

"Sure," Pat said. "Just do it, and do it carefully. With you left hand"

The man slowly opened his jacket. His gun was tucked into the left side of his belt—right handed as Pat had assumed. Using his thumb and finger of his left hand he pulled out the gun and carefully laid it on the ground.

"Toward me." Pat shouted.

"Go fuck yourself," he answered.

Pat handed her gun to Sue and carefully walked over to the gun on the ground. Reaching down for the gun she slid it across the ground toward Sue. She didn't move fast enough and couldn't escape the man's foot as it rose and hit her with all the rage he could muster on the left side of her face. She fell back in agony, feeling the blood run down her face. The pain was intense and she could actually hear bells ringing in her ears. She sat waiting for her head to clear. She wanted to cry and ask for help, but didn't.

Before the man's foot returned from the kick, Sue shot him in his leg. He tumbled to the ground grasping for his leg, cursing everybody and everything he could think of.

Magee stood with his hands above his head, not believing what was happening around him.

"What in God's name are you people doing?" he asked. "Have you no shame?"

Pat stood up holding her face. She took back her gun from Sue and wiping the trickle of blood from her face, re-trained it on her man.

"Take your jacket off." Carolyn said to Magee. "Carefully."

"I don't carry a gun," he answered, slowly removing his jacket.

"If I see one on you, I'll shoot you," Pat said looking at him sideways. "That's a promise. I haven't shot anyone today, and it's my turn."

Magee took off his jacket and put it slowly on the ground.

"We have a problem," Ed warned them, motioning beyond Magee toward the café. A woman was walking straight toward them, clearly unconcerned about what was happening. Her steps were long and quick. She wanted to be seen.

"Who's she?" Carolyn asked Magee.

He didn't need to turn his head. "She's one of us," he grinned. "Are you going to kill an unarmed woman?"

Carolyn lowered her gun to Magee's groin area. "You've got five seconds and then I'll blow them away." She started counting Magee turned his head to call to the lady. "Martina," he shouted, "go back for the love of God. She's threatening to shoot me bloody bollocks off! For God's sake, leave."

The woman stopped, visibly shaken at what was happening. She turned and walked away as quickly as she had arrived.

Carolyn reached into her pocket for her walkie-talkie. "Two ambulances needed," she said. "Three minutes later send in the police." She put the walkie-talkie away without waiting for a response.

Immediately there was a siren of ambulances and within thirty seconds the two men and Pat had emergency personnel working on them.

Carolyn and Ed handcuffed Magee's hands behind his back and helped him into an ambulance. They laid him out on a stretcher, keeping a gun on him at all times.

Police sirens now filled the air. Ed, Sue, Pat and the medic looking after her entered the ambulance with Carolyn and Magee. Carolyn waved down the first police car. A policeman who appeared to be at a senior level spoke briefly to Carolyn as she motioned to the two men, the two guns still on the ground and the dropped cameras. He saluted Carolyn, and started toward the two men.

Carolyn got in the front of the ambulance, and turned to the driver. "Airport please," she said, looking back into the now full working area. "We have a plane to catch."

The medic worked on Pat's face and ensured her, in broken English, that she would be okay.

Pat leaned into the medic to be heard. "Will I have a scar?" she called out.

The medic gestured with her hands. "Maybe small one yes?"

Pat wanted to roll her eyes in despair, but it hurt too much. She smiled at the medic instead, thanking her.

The siren was suddenly turned off. Carolyn turned to face the others. "We are being followed. Mister, check out the rear and see if you can see who it is.

Ed returned quickly from looking. "It's our lady friend Martina"

"That would be Martina Anderson," Pat added quickly. "Full member of the Provisional IRA. She jumped bail three years ago and is believed to have been part of the Brighton bombing. She's no saint!"

"Well done, Boss," Carolyn said, nodding agreement with Pat's summary. "Here's our plan."

They huddled together quickly discussing and reviewing the plan to understand their respective parts.

"And remember," Carolyn summed up, "number one priority is the safety of ourselves and the public."

Moving back into the passenger seat she opened the channel on her walkie-talkie and outlined their situation. Ed moved to the back door and looked out. He waved to Carolyn and the ambulance sped up. The car following picked up speed until it was only a few feet behind them. Ed counted three fingers on his free hand, and on three the driver jammed on the brakes as hard as he could. As expected the car behind rammed into them, sending things flying.

Pat and Carolyn, with their guns drawn, moved quickly out of the passenger door and sped to stand in front of the ambulance.

Ed and Sue dragged Magee to his feet, both keeping their guns against his back. They pushed him to the back door and opened the door just enough for his body to fill the space.

Ed peered carefully around Magee to see the situation. He knew Pat and Carolyn were now edging along either side of the ambulance ready to shoot. The female driver of the car behind was shaking her head to catch her breath. She moved quickly. She opened the driver's side window with her right hand. Her left hand appeared holding a gun. As she held the gun out of the window Sue shouted a warning. Ed pointed his gun at Anderson's head and pulled the trigger.

The windscreen in the car shattered into a thousand pieces exploding with an intense crack. At the explosion a look of fear spread across Martina's face and she screamed a horrifying screech.

"Mary Mother of God Almighty," Magee screamed, "what on earth have you done man?"

After shattering the glass the bullet moved through the car, hit Martina in the forehead creating a small amount of blood then fell harmlessly into her lap. She let her gun drop out the window and sat motionless, wondering if she was, in fact, still alive. She closed her eyes to pray.

Ed thanked any God who was listening. "I think I've just saved her life," he said.

Sue dragged Magee back to the side bed and forcing him face down pushed her gun into his back to make her message clear.

As Carolyn and Pat moved quickly to the car, a police car drew up behind the scene of the accident. The same senior officer from the Dam

Square jumped from the car and ran to see what was happening in his usually peaceful city on a quiet Sunday in June.

Carolyn spoke to him, outlining the situation. He was visibly disturbed and made it clear to Carolyn that he was not used to shoot-outs. This was Amsterdam, not New York City!

Carolyn pointed to Pat, who turned so that her now swollen left eye was obvious. She tried to smile, making it clear to their host that it hurt.

The police officer waved them on. He wanted the street cleared immediately.

Martina Anderson, now handcuffed, was carefully taken into the ambulance. She neither spoke nor made any signs of resistance. It was obvious she was in severe shock. The medic started working with her to calm her nerves.

Pat and Carolyn jumped quickly back into the ambulance and it continued its trip to Amsterdam airport.

Except for the medic speaking quietly and calmly to Anderson, no one spoke.

Ed closed his eyes in order to fully understand what had happened. As he opened them, he saw Carolyn looking at him. She gave him a quick smile, a nod, and mouthed 'well done'.

The ambulance drove through all levels of security at the airport without stopping. It pulled up to the plane they had arrived in a short five hours earlier.

"It seems we have a welcoming party," Carolyn said, pointing to a jeep that was alongside their plane. "U.S. military plates," she continued, looking at Pat. "Will you do the honours, Boss?"

Pat grinned. "Yes, Miss. My pleasure." She put her gun on safety and picked a business card from her purse and slipped the card into her pocket.

As the ambulance came to a stop, Pat exited the back door, looking around carefully as she jumped down. Standing next to the jeep was a tall blond man. He wore a short sleeve shirt and casual pants.

"You won't need the gun," he said, looking at Pat, "I'm American."

"So was Alger Hiss." Pat replied.

"What?" he asked in amazement. "He's a goddamned spy."

"My point exactly," Pat replied.

"Hey I'm CIA," the man responded. "If you'll keep the gun down I'll show you my I.D. It's right here in my shirt pocket."

Pat eyed him suspiciously. "What's the capital of South Dakota?"

He shook his head at the question. "What?"

Pat spoke slowly as if to a child. "I asked you—what is the capital of South Dakota?"

He closed his eyes to think, not expecting an examination. "Bismarck," he answered carefully.

Pat raised her gun and released the safety. "Try again."

He raised both hands. "Whoa, I was just testing you," he stammered. "It's Pierre." He pronounced it 'Peer'. "The capital of South Dakota is Pierre. Put the gun down for Christ's sake!"

Pat lowered her gun. "Sure, no problem." She smiled innocently. "May I see your I.D. please?"

He carefully withdrew his identification wallet and showed her his badge. "I just came to congratulate you," he said, taking out a card and offering it to her. "We were working the airport."

"Thanks," Pat said taking the card. "Can't be too careful nowadays."

He nodded his understanding. "You don't sound British to me."

"I'm from Canada. You know the big pink country above the U.S?"

He smiled. "You mean the Great White North, eh hoser?"

"That's the one," Pat laughed. "But my name's not McKenzie." She reached out and shook his hand. "Pat Weston."

"What happened to your eye? It looks like it hurts."

"Kicked by an Irish gorilla," Pat answered, touching her eye gently. "But he's in hospital nursing a bullet in his leg."

"Ouch," he laughed. "You Canadians are tough."

"The shooter was British; English actually. Nice lady."

He raised his eyebrows. "It gets better as we talk about it."

"All in a day's work."

"Do you have a card?" he asked.

Pat searched her pockets for a card. "I just happen to have one here," she said, passing him her card.

"Export Development Canada. That's clever. Hey look, can I phone you some time?"

She squinted at him, closing her bad eye.

"Just for business, y'know? Hands across the border and all."

"Sure, Robert Lambrick," she answered, looking at his card. "Hands across the border and all."

He got in the jeep. "Congratulations, guys," he called back. "Ya done good!" He started the jeep and left.

Pat turned to the plane. Carolyn was standing by the door with a broad grin on her face. "Hands across the border eh?" They chuckled and entered the plane

The pilot and co-pilot hadn't been expecting one prisoner, let alone two. Magee and Anderson were seated onto the first row of seats. Magee was still handcuffed behind his back. Carolyn considered moving his hands to his front but decided against it. "It's a short trip," she indicated to Magee. Magee said nothing, accepting his fate and considered his situation better than his three comrades. Anderson had been handcuffed with her hands on her lap. She was still noticeably in shock and obviously not a risk to anyone.

Everyone took his or her seat and without delay the plane took off. No one spoke as the plane headed to fifteen thousand feet, its cruising altitude for the short flight.

Sue sat next to Ed and leaned over to speak quietly. "The two others send their regards," she whispered. "The work is going well."

Ed nodded and asked her to say hello to them. Ed had met Sue during Operation Hawfinch when they worked together in Libya. Sue and her associates Lyle Fraser and Mike Sampson were negotiating with the Libyan authorities to get needed medical supplies to Libya, and in return to have oil exported to the U.K. at a reasonable price. Ed had become involved temporarily in the negotiations as a cover to kidnap the soldier who had shot a British policewoman at the Libyan Embassy in London. The soldier, as it turned out, had committed suicide, stabbing himself in the heart and dying silently in front of Ed. Ed still wondered if the operation was a true success. Lord Stonebridge had ensured him that the prime minister considered it a success, and that was what really mattered.

The plane levelled off and Ed moved to the rear of the plane to make coffee. As the aroma filled the compartment, Sue, Carolyn and Pat joined Ed at the table. Pat took coffees to the pilot and co-pilot, spending some time in the cockpit enjoying the view as they crossed the English Channel. As she passed Magee and Anderson she stopped. "I suppose you'd like a coffee?" she asked bluntly.

"Such good manners," he replied with a smile and his strong Irish accent. "How could I say no to such a generous offer? Black with just a touch of sugar please."

Anderson shook her head in silence.

Pat didn't respond to Magee, not wanting to waste her time.

Sue poured the coffee. "I'll take it to him. Perhaps I won't accidentally spill it on him."

Pat agreed with a nod.

"So what makes you want to kill people?" Sue asked as she stood in the aisle by Magee, holding the cup to his lips carefully. He took a long sip.

"Why do the English people think they should govern the Irish people in their own land?"

"I suppose in part," Sue responded, "because the majority of Northern Ireland voters want to be part of Britain. But then as I understand it, you don't want to just take over Northern Ireland, you also want to replace the government in the Republic of Ireland?"

"Of course we do. We want a new socialist government for all of Ireland. The current government has given into the English. We want to start anew. One country, one government."

"But two religions. Surely it doesn't take too much brain power to believe there would be terrible blood-shed if somehow the two entities became one?"

"Religion has nothing to do with it." Magee was now speaking loud enough for all to hear. "The damned Protestants can have their own church. Just as long as they stick to themselves."

"That's very flexible of you," Pat called out.

Magee spat back. "Listen to the damn American bitch. Doesn't she know whose side she should be on? Listen Yank," he called back to Pat, "Reagan is on our side. He's Irish. Even the prime minister of Canada has Irish blood. Things will get better. You'll see!"

Carolyn looked at Pat and nodded to her to continue the conversation.

Pat smiled, and shouted back. "Trudeau's not Irish you idiot!"

Magee laughed. "Typical bloody American," he shouted back. "She doesn't even know what goes on outside of her own country. Mulroney's the bloody prime minister for Christ's sake." He shook his head. "Americans!" he spat in disgust.

Carolyn gave Pat the thumbs up. Pat winked back and took a long sip of her coffee.

Sue leaned over and offered Magee more coffee. When he had finished drinking, she moved back to the rear of the plane. No one spoke, but they were all pleased with the conversation.

Unplanned and out of character, Carolyn took her gun from her purse and walked forward to Magee. Her three team members couldn't believe what happened next. Carolyn held her gun to Magee's head and spoke clearly and slowly. "If you don't cease all and any activity in connection with Mrs. Crowe in Kensal Rise, you're brown bread. Understand?"

Magee nodded silently.

Carolyn returned to her seat and withdrew a note pad from her purse. "That's not part of any report," she said, looking down to start her notes. "Let's say it was personal shall we."

Pat looked at Ed in amazement and mouthed. 'Brown bread?'

Ed ran his hand across his throat and mouthed back. 'Dead.'

The plane started its descent and they each buckled-up for landing.

The plane came to an abrupt stop and Carolyn moved to the front of the plane. "Here's where you get off, sir and madam. Welcome to Scotland."

Magee and Anderson were untied and the plane door was opened. Fifteen feet away a Glasgow police car sat with the back door open.

Carolyn motioned to Ed and Pat. "Boss, Mister, would you escort our guests to the car please?"

Ed and Pat walked Magee and Anderson to the car, helped them in and closed the doors. Ed turned toward the plane, while Pat took the opportunity to make a point. She opened the door by Magee, and looked him squarely in the face. "Remember; brown bread! It'll be my pleasure." She slammed the door closed not waiting for a response. The car quickly drove across the tarmac and disappeared from view.

As they walked toward the plane Carolyn was standing in the doorway with the camera ready. "Smile," she called out. They both smiled, and she took the photograph. Ed and Pat got back into the plane, the door was closed and they took their seats for take off.

"That's not official," Carolyn said to them over the sound of the revving engines, "but I thought you would both like a souvenir of your first trip to Scotland!"

Within minutes of the door closing, everyone was buckled up and ready to go. They sat in their 'usual' seats—Ed next to Sue and Carolyn next to Pat. Other than a few facial expressions between each other, there was no communication. When the plane reached cruising altitude they automatically moved to the rear of the plane, sat at the board table, and Ed put on the coffee.

"Well!" Carolyn started the conversation, "that was quite a day."

"A good day," Pat said enthusiastically. "A damn good day! Good work by the A team."

Sue nodded slowly. "I've never shot anyone before. I hope to hell he lives."

Carolyn leaned over and touched Sue's shoulder. "He will. You shot him in the correct leg."

Sue laughed lightly. "I did? I didn't know there was a difference."

Ed raised his hand to hold off the conversation. "Let's get our coffee brewed. I've got to tell you, I'm sure glad I didn't kill that lady, but that was more luck than judgement."

Carolyn drew herself up to the table and waited as Ed shuffled the cups and poured the coffee. "Here's why I shot the first man," she started, "and why I shot him where I did." They each took a sip of the best tasting coffee they had enjoyed in a few days. "The main reason I shot him was to clear the square. We were in an untenable situation, so I went against my own rule to shoot to kill. I didn't need to kill him, but I needed to send a message to both the public and the three of them."

"Good decision." Sue added quickly.

Carolyn nodded her thanks. "So why his leg, and why his left leg? I wanted the bullet to stop in his body, thereby eliminating the risks of what we so nicely call collateral damage. I picked his left leg because from where I was standing that meant I would hit him on the outside of his leg, where the thigh muscle is larger and furthest from the veins and arteries that are on the inside of our legs, of course."

"Jesus, Carolyn," Pat asked in amazement. "You thought of that all in a matter of seconds? I am truly impressed."

"It seemed to make sense," Carolyn shrugged. "It was more reactive than thoughtful."

Sue smiled, shaking her head. "Hell, I shot my man in the right leg because it was the closest leg available!"

"And I'm glad you did," Pat said, touching her swollen left eye.

They took a few seconds to enjoy the moment of laughter. Then they turned to Ed.

"Obviously men follow instructions better than us women," Carolyn said. "Job well done, Ed. It must have been a difficult decision?" She gave him an extra smile as she spoke.

Ed bit his lip, thinking back to the shooting. "I've got to tell you all, that it wasn't exactly what you might think. I read a story a couple of months ago where a Mountie, up in the north of Canada somewhere, was in the same situation and shot a man through the windscreen of a car. The bullet didn't even reach its target, but the result was the same—a very scared driver. I wasn't sure what would happen, but it seemed to make sense at the time."

"Bloody hell," Sue said. "That was amazing." She paused. "But what would you have done if she hadn't frozen?"

Ed shrugged and pulled a face. "Followed orders."

Pat toasted Ed with her coffee. "Good for you, Ed. We're proud of you. You're okay!" Carolyn and Sue joined in the toast.

"So who's your new American friend?" Sue asked Pat.

Pat waved her off. "Oh, y'know, your typical Yank. Tall, good looking, rich, probably drives two cars and has a second home in California."

Sue raised her eyebrows. "Sounds rather nice to me."

"Does he have any friends?" Carolyn asked.

"Excuse me, ladies," Ed interrupted, "I'm still here you know."

Pat shrugged with a nice smile. "But, Ed, you're a mixture of English and Canadian . . ."

"Pretty boring stuff," Sue added solemnly.

Ed rolled his eyes. "Well excuse me. I'll just sit by myself and read the cricket scores."

"You have your uses, Ed," Carolyn assured him. "Why don't you pour us some more coffee?"

Ed joined in the laughter, but poured more coffee anyway.

Carolyn outlined the plan for the rest of the day. After landing in an un-named airport the four of them would be driven to the Inn. The Inn, Carolyn explained was a private government Inn, secure and safe from intruders. Carolyn would continue on to Stonebridge Manor, give a brief report to Lord Stonebridge, and return to join them for dinner and drinks. The next day they would all report to Lord Stonebridge as a group.

"Questions?" Carolyn asked, just as the plane started its descent.

"I hope you'll stay with us at the Inn tonight," Sue said thoughtfully. "It will be nice to go to the manor tomorrow as a group."

Carolyn agreed. "And Ed, I'll need your gun when I return from the manor later on. It stays at the Inn under lock and key."

Landing smoothly, the plane taxied up to the waiting limousine. After thanking the crew, they scrambled into the limousine like a group of teenagers, all trying for the best seats.

Ed spread his hands wide to Pat. "Welcome to 'jolly old'," he said with a smile.

Pat looked out of the window, pointing. "Thanks. When does it start raining?"

'Soon enough,' her three hosts promised.

Ed, Sue, and Pat exited at the Inn, and waved Carolyn on. Their rooms were ready, and 'dinner would be served at eight o'clock sharp'.

"Well I'm for a hot bath," Sue said as they walked to their rooms.

"I'm for a hot tub," Pat responded, stressing 'tub'.

Ed eyed each one. "I'm going to fill my bathtub with hot water and get in it."

"Always a politician," Sue laughed.

"Wimp!" Pat corrected her.

"Never want to disagree with a lady" Ed said, entering his room.

Ed lingered in his bathtub until the water was cool. He threw on a bathrobe provided by the Inn and turned on the television, hoping to catch the first announcement of the Brighton Bomber. There was nothing about the capture. There was a knock on the door, and without waiting for an answer Pat came into the room.

She smiled at his state of undress. "Can we chat?"

"Be my pleasure, Pat. Coffee, tea?"

She shook her head. "I'll wait for the wine later."

"Chat away," Ed said.

"I'm thinking of quitting my job."

Ed's eyes widened. "Surely not! I thought you liked what we did today."

Pat nodded. "I did. I want to do it more often. I want to do what Carolyn does."

"Okay, I'm confused," Ed said, walking over to make coffee.

"Yes, I know you are. I'm not giving you the full facts. Let me explain." She took a deep breath. "You know why I'm here today, it's because you got involved in the IRA issue somewhat accidentally in Paris."

"Okay, I'm with you so far."

"You're involved; therefore I'm involved at a higher level."

"Got it."

"But, Ed, when I go back to Ottawa, I'm back at my desk. I'm an administrator. I'm not in the field again. This is a one shot deal." She shrugged. "I want it full time. So I'm not really quitting my job, I'm going to put in for a transfer to be a real CSIS operative." She smiled. "What do you think?"

He sat across the room from her, thinking. "A one shot deal?" he grinned.

"Oh, you and your play on words," she chuckled. "Give over will you."

"Can I think about it for a while, Pat? Maybe we could discuss it more on the flight back tomorrow—just the two of us, with plenty of time."

Pat stood and walked toward the door. "Good answer, Ed, we'll talk about it tomorrow." She reached the door and turned. "And, Ed?"

Ed looked up. "Yeah?"

She winked. "Don't sit like that when you're wearing a bathrobe!"

The phone rang at 7:30. Ed picked it up keeping his eye on the television, still waiting for the first news of the arrest in Glasgow.

"Crowe here."

Carolyn couldn't resist it. "Caw, caw," she answered in a high pitch voice.

Ed smiled. "And that from the lady I love."

"Ah, that's nice," Carolyn said sweetly. "Now that *is* something to crow about!"

"I gather the meeting with your . . . Lord Stonebridge went well?"

"Yes, it did," she answered. "Look I'll be ready in ten. Can you drop by with your gun? I'm next door."

"I'll be there in five."

"Ten," she reminded him.

"Seven and a half," he said as he hung up.

Six minutes later he knocked on her door. He held the gun and holster freely so anyone could see his intent.

"Just a moment," Carolyn called through the door. Moments later she opened the door and stepped back.

She was wearing a short black dress that showed her figure and legs beautifully.

"Wow," he exclaimed, closing the door behind him, "you do look nice."

She turned her back to him. "Would you do me up please, sir?" Her voice was flirty. The zipper of her dress was fully down, exposing the top of her panties and her bra strap. Both were black.

Ed admired her body, not sure what to say or do.

"Pleease?" she begged sexily.

Keeping the gun in his left hand he gently, but slowly, zipped up her dress.

She turned, kissed him on his cheek and took the gun from him.

"Why thank you, Mr. Crowe. You have such good manners."

Ed smiled, looking into her eyes. "You have lovely eyes, Miss Andrews, and I love you."

She put her finger to her lips, kissed it and laid it on Ed's lips. "And I love you, Mr. Crowe, but we cannot ruin my make-up. It's taken my forever to put my face on."

Ed held her hand and kissed her finger. "You look lovely even without make-up, Carolyn."

"Leave, Ed, or you'll have me teary."

Ed headed for the door. "I'm going to knock on both of the ladies' door and escort all three of you to dinner."

"You are a gentleman, sir." Carolyn curtsied. "But please don't suggest to Pat that you knocked her up, okay?"

Ed patted the side of his nose. "Yes, your ladyship. I shall return with a damsel on each arm."

The restaurant manager guided them to their table, assisting each lady with their chair. After pouring each of them a glass of white wine, he silently left them to their discussions.

Carolyn raised her glass. "A toast to The A Team."

They raised their glasses. "The A team."

The meal was served and idle chatter took centre stage. Carolyn watched the conversation with special attention. She was pleasantly surprised how well the four of them got along. Four different personalities and backgrounds she realized, yet the four of them were a solid team.

"So ladies," Pat said, bringing the chatter to a halt, "I asked Ed today what he thought of the idea of my moving from my regular desk-bound job to a job in the field. Perhaps Ed you could let us know what you think of the idea?"

Ed wiped his lips with a napkin. "What do I think?"

Pat nodded. "That's the question. What do you think?"

Ed rubbed his chin. "What do you think I might think?"

"So you're asking me," Pat responded slowly, "what do I think you might think about my asking you about my thinking of changing jobs?"

Carolyn and Sue put down their cutlery and lifted their glasses to watch the unanticipated entertainment.

Ed thought briefly. "Well I think that what you think about what I might think about the thought of your changing jobs may adjust my thinking on the question at hand."

Pat closed one eye to consider his point. "I think I see what you're thinking," she said. "You seem to think that what I think about what you think about the thought of my thoughts on changing jobs may affect your thinking. Is that what you think you're thinking?"

"Yes," Ed said.

"Yes what?"

"Yes to what you just said."

Pat rolled her eyes. "I don't even know what I just said."

Ed grinned. "What you just said . . ."

Carolyn raised her hand. "Hold it, hold it. Enough! My meal is getting cold." She turned to Ed. "Should Miss Weston change jobs? And please be monosyllabic in your response."

Ed considered the question, chewing on his bottom lip. He finally responded.

"Maybe!"

"Dear, God," Carolyn groaned. "I'm ready to go get my gun!"

Sue interrupted with a laugh. "Perhaps, Ed you could expand on your answer? I suspect it is deeper than it might appear."

"It is actually," Ed said, sitting straighter. "Personally, Pat, I know you'd do a super job in the field. You have a wonderful approach to life—what I would call firm but fair. No one I know works as hard as you or as intelligently as you. You'd be a great field operative, no questions asked."

Pat stared at Ed, not able to clear her throat to respond. She was stuck for words.

"But?" Carolyn asked.

"But," Ed continued, "there's always a 'but'. My mother doesn't know of my additional responsibilities as a consultant to MI6, and I hope she never finds out. I do, however, know of one mother, who is aware of her daughter's field activities, or at least the risks involved, and I doubt she sleeps easy at night." He turned to Pat. "I just suspect your mother would put two and two together and come up with the right answer. Besides," he added, "who'd look after Robin?"

Pat excused herself and walked quickly to the ladies' rest room.

"Wow," Sue exclaimed. "I don't think we were expecting an answer like that."

"I know I wasn't," Carolyn admitted. She stood and followed Pat into the ladies' room.

Ed turned to Sue. "I have to tell the truth don't I?"

Sue nodded. "Absolutely. To do otherwise would be unfair to Pat in her decision making process."

Five minutes later Carolyn and Pat re-joined the table laughing and carrying-on like life-long friends.

Pat raised her glass. "I'd like to toast a really nice bloke, a good guy, and a very good friend. To Ed."

Sue and Carolyn joined in the toast.

Ed smiled his thanks, glad that he hadn't put his foot too deeply into his mouth.

Pat smiled at the three of them. "I'm putting in for a transfer as soon as I return to the office."

Nothing further was said about Pat's decision. They finished their meal, limiting the discussion to small talk—anything but their activities of the day. By ten-thirty exhaustion had taken over. Carolyn up-dated them noting that their luggage would be outside their rooms when they awoke in the morning. After agreeing to be ready to leave by eight-thirty the next morning they returned to their rooms, each to review the success of the day in their own way.

Ed was asleep within minutes.

Sue tried to read a book, and fell asleep with the light on.

Pat sat for a while with an ice bag to her swollen left eye.

Carolyn started to complete her report for the next day, but gave up. She set the alarm for six-thirty.

CHAPTER TWENTY

MONDAY, JUNE 24TH 1985

• • • • • • •

E d was up dressed and ready to go at seven-thirty. To his surprise
he was the last one at the breakfast table. The three ladies were
sitting at a table for four sharing a large pot of tea.

He waved as he walked to them. "Early birds, eh?"

The response was three dirty looks.

"No play on words intended," he said, taking the empty seat. "Let
me restate that. Early risers get the tea, eh?"

All three now smiled and wished him a good morning.

"And thanks for getting our bags to us, Carolyn. Nice to be wearing
fresh underwear, right ladies?"

Three sets of eyes rolled, and he got no verbal response.

"I'm just saying!" he added.

"Don't bother, Ed," Pat replied on behalf of the ladies. "Before you
got here we were enjoying a nice cup of tea and discussing the lovely
flowers in the garden, not the state of your personal dress."

He poured himself a cup of tea.

Carolyn moved up to the table and took command. "Here's the plan
for the day. We leave here at eight-thirty. I know Lord Stonebridge is
busy on the phone for a few hours so we'll take a slow, scenic drive to
Stonebridge Manor and show off some of our famous countryside to Pat.
There will be the obligatory visit with Lady Stonebridge." She turned
to Pat. "You're the only person she doesn't know, Pat, so be ready to
outline your personal life in a sentence or two."

Pat winced at the thought.

Ed spoke up. "A tad of an exaggeration perhaps, Pat. But it is Lady Stonebridge I was referring to last night as a nervous mother."

"I think she's a super lady," Sue added. "And that's with both a large L and a small L."

Carolyn smiled and continued. "We will then meet with Lord Stonebridge and the General to make our verbal reports." Carolyn explained to Pat who 'the General' was, and how Lord Stonebridge used the General's experience and common-sense approach to life in dealing with many activities in the department.

"I would suggest we take turns in the verbal report," Carolyn said, looking for agreement which she received—if only grudgingly from Pat. Carolyn assured her that the hardest part would be over by the time they got to Lord Stonebridge's office.

"And after the verbal report to Lord Stonebridge," Carolyn said with a sad look, "we can all head for home. Won't that be nice?"

The blank response to her question made it clear no one wanted the excitement to end that quickly.

At exactly eight-thirty the limousine left the Inn with the four team members, now pleasantly excited. The weather was cool with just a few clouds in the sky. Carolyn spoke to the driver about a bit of a tour for 'our Canadian guest'.

The limousine turned left as it exited the Inn, and headed south. Carolyn outlined the historical and interesting sites to Pat, who took in everything with a passion. For almost an hour the tour kept strictly to the back roads, with some of them barely wide enough for one vehicle.

"That is Chequers," Carolyn pointed out, "the country home of the prime minister." Little could be seen from the road, and any security personnel were well hidden. The limousine pulled onto a busier road and headed north.

Pat pointed to a small number of houses and a church as they passed by. "What's the name of this village?" Pat asked. "It is so pretty."

"Little Kimble," Carolyn answered, careful not to look toward Ed.

Ed looked out of the window just as they passed The Sun Inn. His heart skipped a beat. This was the pub, he realized, where he had committed to ask Carolyn to marry him—on October 29th 1989; just a little over four years from now. He looked back through the rear window to capture one last view of the pub.

"Nice looking pub," he said, not turning to catch Carolyn's reaction.

"What's wrong with The Queen's Head?" Pat asked.

"Nothing, nothing at all," Ed replied. "This one just looks a little cozier. Nice place, Carolyn?"

"I haven't visited it too often" Carolyn said. "I'm told it's a nice place for a quiet drink and relaxing conversation." She grinned at Ed. "Here we are," she announced as the limousine turned through the gates into Stonebridge Manor.

"Holy crap," was all Pat could manage.

The maid opened the door and directed them toward the drawing room. Pat lingered behind wondering if the foyer and stairway area in the manor wasn't larger than her entire apartment in Ottawa. She followed the rest into the drawing room—or the interrogation room!

Lady Stonebridge stood and welcomed her guests. Carolyn introduced Pat as the 'other' Canadian member. They were all seated with Lady Stonebridge taking her regular center spot. On the table in front of her was that morning's copy of the Telegraph, with a larger than usual heading; 'Brighton Bomber Arrested in Glasgow.'

Lady Stonebridge turned to Pat. "so tell me, Miss Weston, how could such a pretty lady such as you get such a shiner?"

Pat smiled in spite of the pain. "Very silly of me, Lady Stonebridge, I walked into a door."

Lady Stonebridge looked at the newspaper and then at Pat. "A Scotch Pine door no doubt?"

Carolyn became nervous.

"It was Dutch Elm actually," Pat responded with the nicest of smiles.

Lady Stonebridge was taken aback, and waved off the discussion. "And there I thought that was a disease," she muttered.

Carolyn's concern abated as the maid entered the room with the tea trolley. Tea was poured and everyone returned to their seats.

"I must say," Lady Stonebridge continued, "you all look very pleased with yourselves. A successful trip was it?"

Carolyn was about to reply, but Pat responded.

"We had a lovely trip in this morning," she said enthusiastically. "England's countryside is as beautiful as it is made out to be. Carolyn took us on a wonderful tour, and we even drove by Chequers. And we drove through a very pretty village with the charming name of Little Kimble."

Lady Stonebridge knew when to admit defeat. "Yes that is a very pretty village," she said, sipping her tea. "It has a most charming church and once in a while we attend a wedding there. It is so perfect; for a wedding that is."

Lady Stonebridge turned back to Pat. "So what do you do in Ottawa, Miss Weston? I assume you work for the government?"

"I work for Export Development Canada," Pat replied. "I help the private sector sell goods to countries around the world. My main goal is to help with all of the red tape."

"Very good, very good," Lady Stonebridge answered. "A government helping the private sector is indeed a novel idea. We all need more of that."

The conversation continued about the world economy with Lady Stonebridge taking the lead.

"We must head up now, Mother," Carolyn said, smiling dutifully. "Duty calls."

Lady Stonebridge conceded. "As you say, dear. Do have a fine meeting."

Everyone thanked Lady Stonebridge and headed for the door.

"A moment alone, Mr. Crowe?" Lady Stonebridge asked.

Carolyn glanced at her. "Mother!"

"In private please," Lady Stonebridge smiled.

Ed stayed behind and closed the door. "Yes Mrs. S?"

"Not everyone needs to know everything, Edwin. We do have private lives." She sat straight. "I saw your mother on Saturday. I wanted you to know we had a fine old chat; you know, about children and everything."

Ed understood. "Of course, it was Ascot week. It slipped my mind. I'm sure she enjoyed your visit."

"We enjoyed each other's company, and your mother was good enough to invite her neighbors for a couple of photographs. My hat was a bit of a hit."

"I'm sure it was. I suspect I'll see the photos shortly."

"Well that was all, Edwin. It would have been rude of me not to tell you. Do have a good meeting."

Ed bowed his head. "Thank you, Lady Stonebridge," he said deliberately using her full title. He left the room and ran up-stairs to Lord Stonebridge's office.

Pat had been introduced and they waited for Ed to begin the meeting.

Mr. Cooper stood and shook hands with Ed. "You're looking good, Eddie," he said with a smile.

Lord Stonebridge shook Ed's hand with a firm grasp. "Nice to see you again, Mr. Crowe, especially under the circumstances."

Lord Stonebridge walked behind his desk, which was scattered with files and note pads. He cleaned the desk as best he could and ordered tea for eight, knowing there were only six, but a thirsty six.

"Ladies and gentlemen," Lord Stonebridge began, "let me say that I have just spent a considerable amount of time on the phone with our prime minister. Now I think it's fair to say that the past weeks and months have been difficult for any politician, especially those that were in Brighton at the time of the bombing. The prime minister has taken the entire matter personally and handled it directly with me. Today, I am glad to report, I can say she is gratified with our activities. I would like to say 'happy', but that would denigrate the circumstances that brought us here today in the first place."

Mr. Cooper sensed Lord Stonebridge was struggling with his remarks. "I would say, sir, if I may, that I suspect the people in the room are only too happy, and I use that word carefully, to have helped in bringing this one item of a much larger plan to fruition."

The comment brought a small but meaningful round of applause that helped settle the nerves of everyone.

Lord Stonebridge took a deep breath. "Thank you, General. It is at times like this that I recognize your special talents in understanding human nature." He sat straighter in his chair, looked over his glasses at each of them, and continued. "To business then! Miss Andrews I understand you have an agreed-upon process for your verbal report."

"Yes, sir. I will start, to be followed by Miss Banks, then Mr. Crowe, and finally Miss Weston will play clean-up: as they say in baseball."

Tea was delivered and served.

Carolyn started her report outlining the agreed-upon plan, their aliases, 'shoot-to-kill' orders, and the name The A Team. Lord Stonebridge and Mr. Cooper took notes, asking important questions as she reported.

Sue took over at the point when they got off the plane in Amsterdam to when Carolyn shot the first man in the leg.

"Oh my!" Mr. Cooper exclaimed.

"Shoot to kill?" Lord Stonebridge asked reluctantly.

Carolyn explained her reasoning, which was accepted readily and taken down in detail by both Lord Stonebridge and Mr. Cooper. "Something to bear in mind," Mr. Cooper summed up.

Ed continued the report. Shortly Lord Stonebridge raised a question. "So when you say Miss Weston lowered her gun to his groin area, exactly what do you mean when you say she warned him not to move?"

Pat groaned and looked to the ceiling, hoping it would fall in on her.

Ed had expected the question. "Well, sir, she warned him that if he moved she would, 'transport his testicles into the near future.'" He somehow maintained a straight face.

Lord Stonebridge maintained a business-like approach. "Just like Captain James Kirk of the Spaceship Enterprise?"

Carolyn jumped in. "Absolutely, sir. Just like that other famous Canadian."

Pat had covered her face with her hands, not wanting to be seen.

"I think, General," Lord Stonebridge mused, "we should consider that audible warning for our training program. It seems to have worked wonderfully well for Miss Weston. Twice!"

"Oh God," Pat groaned.

Lord Stonebridge smiled a fatherly smile. "We search for results, Miss Weston, not processes. I like your style."

"Thank you, sir," Pat managed, sitting a bit higher in her seat.

Ed carried on relating the circumstances and was stopped again as he explained Pat being kicked in her face.

"And no one went to her aid?" Mr. Cooper asked.

Pat interrupted in a clear voice. "Absolutely not!" she said. "That would have been out of order and quite unnecessary, Mr. Cooper . . . I mean General."

"You're absolutely correct," Lord Stonebridge agreed. "I think the General was making sure no one put everything at risk by doing so."

"Oh!" Pat mumbled. "Sorry. I jumped to conclusions."

Pat took over the report from when they had left Dam Square with Magee in the ambulance. She understood she was going to describe a touchy part of the report, the shooting of Martina Anderson. She took her time, making sure it was clear that Anderson was moving her gun out of the window and into a position where she could shoot along the side of the ambulance.

"And who was on that side," Lord Stonebridge asked.

It was only then that Ed realized he didn't know, and hadn't asked, whether it was Pat or Carolyn who was at risk.

"I was," Carolyn answered. "Miss Weston and I agreed that I was likely a better shot."

Pat continued the report through to transferring Magee and Anderson to the Glasgow police.

"Let's top up our tea," Lord Stonebridge suggested.

As if planned to the second, as everyone sat to continue the meeting the door opened and the maid wheeled in a trolley with a large cake.

"For our special occasion," Lord Stonebridge announced, walking around his desk to meet the trolley. The cake was large and decorated with a Union Jack, the Canadian Maple Leaf, and the greeting:

Congratulations—The 'Eh' Team

Everyone in the room cheered at the sight of the cake, with Pat having to hold back a very happy tear. Lord Stonebridge presented Pat with the knife and asked her to cut the cake.

"But a photo first," Mr. Cooper announced.

Sue, Carolyn, Pat, and Ed stood around the cake with Pat holding the knife, ready to cut. Mr. Cooper took a photo, using the standard 'cheese' to get an even wider smile than the team members already wore.

"Only five copies will be made," Lord Stonebridge announced. "One for each of you, and one for me. Ed's copy will be sent via Miss Weston in Ottawa. You cannot be too security conscious now days."

The cake was cut and eagerly taken by everyone to his or her seat to enjoy with their cups of tea.

"Wonderful," Pat mumbled through the cake. "Thank you for the treat."

"I will share my photo with the prime minister," Lord Stonebridge added. "I know she will be pleased to see a copy. And by the way, Miss Weston," he added, looking at Pat, "she will be phoning Mr. Mulroney to thank him for all of the support."

"Wow," Pat giggled. "I've never represented my country in this way before. I feel very proud to do so."

"And well deserved," Carolyn added. She turned to Lord Stonebridge. "I know you can't tell us a great deal, sir, but is there anything you can tell us about your conversation with Mrs. Thatcher this morning?" She took a bite of her cake.

Lord Stonebridge considered the question. "She was disappointed in the shooting of Martina Anderson."

Carolyn almost choked on her cake as she stood to make her point, swallowing the cake quickly to catch her breath. "I can't believe that," she protested. "It was a matter of life or death . . ."

Lord Stonebridge smiled and waved her to sit. "As I was saying, the prime minister wondered if we have the right kind of hand guns if car windows can reduce their capacity in such a way as it did yesterday."

Carolyn coughed to clear her throat and calm her nerves. "I'm sorry, sir. I shouldn't have blown up like that." She sat down. "Although you did seem set me up!"

He nodded and winked at her. "I think I did, didn't I?"

Mr. Cooper delicately raised the question of Mrs. Crowe and whether or not the matter regarding the photograph and the warning was still an issue.

Lord Stonebridge's response was interrupted by Pat.

"That is no longer an issue," Pat said quickly, catching everyone's attention. "I told him he'd be brown bread if anything happened to Mrs. Crowe."

Lord Stonebridge looked around the room for help.

"London slang, sir," Mr. Cooper said, almost laughing. "Brown bread—dead."

"You threatened to kill him?" Lord Stonebridge asked turning to Pat.

"Yes I did, sir."

Carolyn motioned to speak, but Pat raised her hands to stop her.

"When he was in the police car in Glasgow, I let him know what would happen to him. He understood." She looked around the room. "I know that can't be part of the official report, but what the hell! It's not like he's a nice guy or anything."

Lord Stonebridge closed his eyes to think, not sure what to say.

Mr. Cooper took over. "So, that's done then. No mention in the report." He paused. "Although, sir, the PM might be interested with a word in her ear?"

Lord Stonebridge nodded. "No doubt, General, no doubt."

With the verbal report finalized Lord Stonebridge and Mr. Cooper shook hands with them conveying their personal congratulations.

"And so to home!" Pat said; now ready to call it a day.

Lord Stonebridge raised his hand. "Miss Weston, Miss Banks, if you would be interested, I'd be happy to give you the twenty minute tour of Stonebridge Manor? We do have a bit of history to tell about."

They both said they would be delighted, and Lord Stonebridge walked them to the door. "Perhaps, General, you could review the details of the written report with Mr. Crowe and Miss Andrews? We shall return in twenty."

Mr. Cooper waited a minute and walked to the door. He turned and bowed. "I'll be back in nineteen." He closed the door quietly as he left.

They were standing ten feet apart, smiling at each other like mischievous kids.

"I love you," Ed said.

"Yes, I know."

"You did a wonderful job. I think your father is very proud of you."

She smiled. "Yes, I think he is."

"Will you be going back to Paris?"

"Only to clean up. The department wants me relocated to a new city."

"Do you know which one?"

She shook her head. "No I don't. And Ed, what are you doing over there when I'm over here? If you were a gentleman . . ."

He walked to her and pulled her gently into his arms, kissing her forehead. Moving down he kissed her lips gently at first and then fiercely, holding her as tightly as he could without hurting her. Carolyn clung to him like it was the last time they would ever kiss.

She looked up at him. "I wanted to join you last night, but it wouldn't have been right. I love you so much."

"When you get to your new city will you let me know where? I will do everything to get to see you soon. I desperately want to make love to you."

Carolyn shivered at the thought. "You'll be the first to know."

They sat down, holding hands.

"Personal question?" Carolyn asked.

"Honest answer." Ed replied.

"What did my mother want to talk to you about?"

"She told me that she dropped in to see my mum on Saturday on the way to Ascot."

Carolyn nodded. "That was nice of her. I'll be sure to thank her."

"So you didn't get to show my mum your fancy hat?"

"No, but it isn't that fancy anyway. Maybe I'll drop in and show it to her some time."

"That would be wonderful. She likes you." He paused. "Personal question?"

Carolyn smiled. "Honest answer."

"What did you and Pat talk about in the ladies' rest room yesterday?"

"I'm not going to tell you."

"Hey," Ed said with surprise, "that's not an honest answer!"

"Yes it is. I'm honestly not going to tell you."

"Okay, you got me there." He kissed her hands. "I know we agreed not to talk about it, but . . ."

Carolyn interrupted. "But only one-thousand-five-hundred and ninety-six days to go before you ask me to marry you."

"At The Sun Inn in Little Kimble," he confirmed.

Carolyn squeezed his hands. "I was almost in shock when Pat talked about brown bread. I was unsure what I would have said. She saved my bacon, for sure. I won't mention it today, but I'll phone her next week and thank her. She's quite a lady."

"Yes she is," Ed agreed with a chuckle. "And she likely meant it too. Unlike you, that is."

Carolyn slowly shook her head. "Oh, I meant it alright. There are rules to play by, and involving family is not part of the game."

Not really sure if she meant what she had said, and not wanting to consider the matter seriously Ed kissed her gently, then holding her tightly he whispered, "Sun Inn, Little Kimble."

With three minutes to go, they sat across the room from one another and talked about where Carolyn might be transferred.

Mr. Cooper arrived on time. Lord Stonebridge and his tour guests returned a minute later.

CHAPTER TWENTY ONE

•‧●●●●‧•

Lord Stonebridge had a large envelope in his hand as he walked around his desk. He looked at it, and then at the people gathered. His look told them something was important.

He held up the envelope. "From the Amsterdam police." He rubbed his chin. "I wonder what it could be."

"There is a way to find out, sir," Sue said subtly.

Carolyn sucked on her lower lip. "Not arrest warrants I hope."

Slowly Lord Stonebridge slit open the envelope and withdrew the contents. "Well, I'll be . . ." He shook his head. "Come see what we have here, General."

Mr. Cooper walked behind the desk and looked over Lord Stonebridge's shoulder. "Well I'll be . . ." he exclaimed.

"Nice angle don't you think, General," Lord Stonebridge asked, pointing at the contents.

"Sir," Carolyn said loudly, "that's not fair!"

Ed, Pat, and Sue nodded in agreement, but held their tongues.

Lord Stonebridge, enjoying the moment, held up two large photos for all to see.

"Oh my God," Pat squealed. "The Japanese tourists!"

The photos clearly showed the four team members holding their guns on Magee and his bodyguards. The only difference in the two photos was in the second photo Carolyn's gun was trained on the bodyguard's leg.

"Now there's a photo to keep," Ed muttered. "A moment later Miss Andrews shot him!"

"These, I am assured by a note form Chief van Wijngaarden," Lord Stonebridge said, holding a sheet of note paper, "are the only copies made." He smiled, uncharacteristically wide. "Mrs. Thatcher will most certainly appreciate these."

While the photos were shared and enthusiastically viewed, Lord Stonebridge took the opportunity to read the full contents of the note from Chief Dirk van Wijngaarden.

"Before we wrap things up," Lord Stonebridge interjected over the buzz, "perhaps you would like an update from Amsterdam?"

Everyone took their seat.

Lord Stonebridge summed up the note. "It seems our two hospitalized friends are doing fine medically, both being well guarded in a special ward. They will both be accused of carrying illegal weapons, a most serious crime in the Netherlands. Miss Anderson, should she ever return, will be arrested for possession of controlled explosives." He folded the note. "More good news, ladies and gentlemen."

"Semtex?" Mr. Cooper asked.

"The IRA's weapon of choice." Lord Stonebridge confirmed. "Now unless there are other items for discussion," he said standing, "I suggest you all go home with the knowledge that you did a wonderful job and can rest assured the appropriate actions for Mr. Magee and Miss Anderson are well under way."

Just as everyone was ready to move, the phone rang. Lord Stonebridge motioned for them to sit and picked up the phone.

"Stonebridge," he answered bluntly. He nodded to the room. "Hello, Ted, how are you? . . . Glad to hear it . . . Yes it went very well . . . She'll be more than happy . . . Yes she phoned Mulroney . . . Yes . . . Yes . . . Yes, I'll put her on." He offered the phone to Pat. "Call for you, Miss Weston."

Pat's face went white as a ghost. She walked to Lord Stonebridge's desk, swallowing hard and licking her lips to speak. Before she spoke she took a deep breath.

"Good afternoon, sir," she said. "Or it's still good morning for you, sir . . . Yes, thank you, sir . . . Very well, yes, sir . . . Oh really? . . . I'm fine, sir . . . As soon as I'm back at my desk, yes . . . I will pass on your message to him right away, sir . . . Thank you, sir . . . Bye now." She hung up the phone, and tried to smile as she walked back to her chair. As she sat down Carolyn topped up Pat's tea and handed it to her.

Lord Stonebridge addressed the room. "As was obvious to Miss Weston, ladies and gentlemen, that was Ted Morden the Director of CSIS in Ottawa. But I'll let Miss Weston fill us in." He looked at Pat who had now regained her composure.

Pat spoke slowly to ensure she didn't miss anything. "That was my boss's, boss's, boss. I've seen him, but never met him." She paused to collect her thoughts. "He wanted me to pass on his congratulations to everyone, and say how pleased he was we could be part of Operation Tea Party. He wanted me to tell you, Ed, that if you are ever bored with working for MI6, he'll be glad to talk to you." She laughed. "Like your life is boring! And the big news, and this is confidential of course, is that Canada's guest from Ed's kidnapping, Mr. Griffin, is being flown from Ottawa to Dublin tonight to be released."

"As the saying goes," Mr. Cooper proffered, "I wouldn't want to be in his shoes."

"Oh, and one more thing," Pat said, now enthusiastically. "When I get back to Ottawa, I'm to give him a call to meet with him and his senior officers." She laughed. "Wow, am I nervous or what?"

"You'll do fine, Pat," Sue said. "Just remember you represent the future of CSIS."

The meeting ended with the shaking of hands and a few high-fives. Lord Stonebridge and Mr. Cooper spend a few moments with each team member thanking and congratulating them again individually.

Somewhat solemnly Pat, Sue, Ed, and Carolyn walked downstairs and out of the front door. The limousine was waiting for them.

Carolyn hugged each of them, thanking them personally as she did. "We made a great team. If we get together again, the first rounds on me." She choked back a tear. "The driver will take Pat and Ed to the airport and then drive you home, Sue."

As they got in the limousine they waved back to Carolyn. The limousine pulled away, leaving Carolyn on the steps of the Stonebridge Manor. As if to reflect the circumstances, it started to rain.

Ed looked over to Pat, catching her wiping away a tear from her good eye. She pointed at him to eliminate any commentary. "Not a dickie bird!"

"Not a word," he agreed.

The clouds moved in and the rain now poured.

Pat sniffed the air. "Smells fresh."

"Smells wet to me," Sue added, peering out of the window. She turned to Pat. "So tell me something about yourself, Pat. What did you do wrong to end up with a job like this?"

Pat chuckled at the question and enjoyed reflecting back on the process that resulted in her current role. Both Sue and Ed listened intently as she described her attending university a year ahead of her peers, and the resulting loneliness that she resolved by being the best, studying more, and getting higher grades than anyone in her graduating year.

"So the federal government sought you out?" Sue asked.

Pat nodded. "Being totally bilingual made it that much easier too. This was still the Trudeau years where bilingualism was of huge importance in hiring employees in the government, or anywhere else for that matter."

Sue nodded her understanding. "Any significant other, if I may ask."

Pat smiled, closed her eyes and rocked her head from side to side, thinking how to respond. "At the risk of sounding like a politician, Sue, I would have to say yes . . . and no."

Sue noticed the reluctance. "Sorry, didn't mean to . . ."

Pat waved her off, deciding to answer the question that she knew would be asked time and time again. "That's okay," she said. "There is a guy that's important to me: very important actually. It's just that our worlds don't fit, not even close. When we do get together it's a great fit, but that's only once in a while."

"Nice guy then?"

Ed swallowed hard and closed his eyes.

"Yeah he's a nice guy, or a good bloke as some might say."

To Ed's relief the limousine pulled into the airport and drove across the tarmac to their plane.

"Rain's stopping," Ed announced.

"Good timing," Pat said.

"Very good timing," Ed agreed.

Pat and Ed collected their bags and after agreeing to keep in touch with Sue, ran through the rain and onto the plane. As they turned to wave goodbye, the limousine was already exiting the airport. Taking their seats, the pilot started the engines and ten minutes later they left the ground heading quickly through the clouds and into a clear blue sky.

As was now his role, after the plane leveled off Ed moved to the rear to make coffee.

Pat looked back from her aisle seat. "Okay with my answers?"

Leaving the coffee to brew he walked to Pat, leaned down and kissed her forehead. "Okay and appreciated," he answered. He sat down across from Pat. "About the brown bread . . ."

"What about it?" Pat shot back. "I told the truth . . ." she paused. "Maybe not the truth, the whole truth, and nothing but the truth so help me God, but then I wasn't in a witness stand, was I?"

"I think that was very clever, tricky, and very, very much appreciated by Carolyn. Well done. End of discussion. Come on back and I'll treat you to you a coffee."

"Well there's a 'come up and I'll show you my etchings' offer if I ever heard one." She unbuckled and joined Ed at the rear table.

Ed poured four coffees and Pat took the pilots' theirs. She returned with a grin. "I think I'll learn how to fly. How about you?"

Ed sipped his coffee. "Not a chance, but good for you. Moving into field operations, thinking of learning to fly, that's quite a dramatic potential change in life-style."

She winked at him. "More than that, I'm not a twenty-five year old virgin any more!"

"Well I'm glad I helped out on that one."

"So am I," Pat grinned. "Listen, can we talk about some personal stuff?"

"Can't get much more personal than talking about losing your virginity can we?"

"Maybe," Pat answered, sipping her coffee.

Ed motioned for her to continue.

"So this CIA guy. The one at Amsterdam airport. What if he, y'know?"

Ed scratched his head. "What if he what?"

"You know what I mean. What if he phones me and we get along and blah, blah, blah."

"Could you be a bit more descriptive here?"

"Christ, Ed, you know what I damn well mean. What if he wants to sleep with me?"

Ed looked at her and smiled. "Well to start I'd say he's got a pretty good taste in women."

"Don't make this awkward for me, Ed. What I'm trying to ask you is if I meet a guy, any guy, where do *we* stand? I don't even like the thought of sleeping with any one but you, but now you've helped me enjoy sex, well . . ."

"Forgive me, Pat," Ed said, reaching over to take her hand, "I really didn't catch on there. Let me top-up our coffees and think this one through."

Pat slid over her cup. "I'm not asking you to marry me, Ed, or anything like that. I know that's not going to happen. Beside, I'm not sure I'd marry you even if you did ask for real. I'm just wondering how long our current most enjoyable relationship might last."

Ed added milk to their coffees and slid her cup across the table to her. He closed his eyes to think. The temptation to lie was immense but he could not, or would not, lie to her.

He opened his eyes. "I guess I'd say about four years."

Pat spilled her coffee as she re-acted verbally and emotionally. "Where the Christ does that come from? You think you're going to have sex with me for four more years and then just dump me? Who the hell do you think you are?"

Ed quickly wiped up the spilled coffee and, taking his time, re-filled her cup.

Pat sat with her hands clenched together in front of her, not bothering to wipe the tears from her face. "You're a sonovabitch, Ed."

Ed spoke quietly. "I'm not, Pat, honest. You asked me a strange question, and I gave you as honest an answer as I could."

Pat glared at him. "Fuck off. Just fuck off. Okay?"

He left the table, walked to the washroom and returned with several tissues. He put them on the table between them and sat back in his seat. Pat picked up the tissues and wiped her face.

He leaned forward. "Are you thinking of babies and that sort of thing?"

"No!"

"What about marriage?"

Her voice calmed. "Not really."

"Then can I ask why you're so mad at me?"

She shook her head. "I don't know. I just don't know how you could come up with an answer like that off the top of your head. You may not be a son of a bitch, but you're damn weird."

"Hey, you're the one that asked the weird question."

"True."

"Do you want to end our relationship now?"

"Of course not, you ass. Why would I want to do that?"

He rolled his eyes and gestured confusion. "Maybe Mr. CIA is Mr. Right?"

"He's American for crying out loud. You don't marry Americans! Jesus, haven't you learned anything yet as a Canadian?"

"Just a dumb D.P. I guess." He paused. "And my name's not Jesus."

"Oh, shut up," she laughed. She grabbed her bag. "I'm going to freshen up." Throwing back the dregs of her coffee, she grabbed her bag and left for the washroom.

Ed scratched his head, wondering why women were so difficult to understand.

When Pat returned she had changed into a heavy T-shirt and shorts. She put away her bag and faced Ed. "Give me a hug please," she asked.

Ed stood, put his arms around her and automatically slipped his hands under the back of her T-shirt.

"Oh my," he whispered. "No bra."

Pat turned around and his hands rested on her breasts. He squeezed them softly, rubbing each nipple with his thumbs.

She leaned her head back and kissed his chin. "This is my way of saying sorry, Ed. I want you to be my lover until either one of us calls it quits, okay?"

"You have lovely breasts Pat. Can I kiss them?"

She turned to face him and lifted her T-shirt. "Quickly," she murmured. He kissed and licked her breasts as she watched him. When she was almost ready to undress him and have sex on the table, she lifted his head to her face and kissed his lips. "Let's continue this on the cruise."

"Deal," he smiled.

They sat down across the aisle from each other. He reached out and took her hand.

"So you wouldn't say yes if I did ask you to marry me?"

"Shut up, Ed."

"Heck, you raised the subject."

She squeezed his hand to hurt him. "Shut up."

He pouted. "I think my feelings are hurt."

"I still have Mr. CIA's business card. Maybe I will phone him and see if he wants to visit me in Ottawa."

"Maybe he could join us on the cruise?" Ed pondered. "Not all Americans are bad are they?"

She pulled her hand away. "Yuck. I'm not into that threesome stuff." She looked at him. "Have you ever . . . ?"

He pulled a face. "Do you mind? I'm still British after all."

She reached over and took his hand. "Can we put this behind us, Ed? Can we go back to twenty minutes ago and forget my stupid comments?"

He leaned over and kissed her hand. "Of course we can. But just you wait until I get you on the cruise!"

She squeezed his hand. "We'll see who gets who."

"Whom," he corrected her.

She let go of his hand. "Listen, Edwin, next time you want to kiss young lady's breasts, be sure to use the correct auxiliary verb. You don't ask '*Can* I kiss them?' since that relates to capabilities, and surely we know you are capable of kissing breasts. The question should be '*May* I kiss them?' since this relates to permission or possibility. I assume you do get permission, verbal or otherwise, before you proceed to kiss young lady's breasts. Are you with me here?"

Ed chuckled. "I apologize. You are absolutely correct!"

"And further to correct English," Pat continued, "you don't need to add the word 'absolutely' to your last sentence, since it is irrelevant. I'm either correct or I'm not correct, there is no need to add a value measurement." She grinned a friendly grin.

Ed knew when he was beaten. "I think I'd better stop speaking."

"Good idea."

"And I was going to tell you I love you!"

183

"So tell me."

He shrugged. "My English is so bad, I'll probably get it wrong."

"Try it!"

"I don't know . . ."

She reached over and punched his arm. "It's three words for crying out loud. Tell me!"

He paused, thinking. He smiled nicely. "You love I."

She gapped in horror. "You bugger. That's the only combination of those three words that make it the opposite!"

"Technically it's not the opposite," he advised her.

She gave him a dirty look. "Don't mess with me. Remember what I did to the last man that didn't follow my orders."

"That should be 'who' didn't . . ." he corrected her, but then quickly added, "I love you."

She smiled and closed her eyes. "Hmmmm. I think I'll take a nap on that."

Ed moved from the aisle seat to the window seat. "Come on over," he called to her. "At least we can sleep side by side."

Pat moved across the aisle, buckled up and took his hand. Without speaking, she kissed his hand tilted her seat back and closed her eyes. Ed tilted his seat and closed his eyes. Within minutes they were both asleep, exhausted from the two day's experience.

Pat kissed Ed gently on the lips to wake him up. He extended the kiss by placing his hands on the back of her neck.

"Coffee's ready," she said. "We arrive in Toronto in half an hour."

Ed joined her at the rear table. The coffee was strong and hot. He took a long sip, enjoying both the taste and the knowledge that the 'A' team had fulfilled its role and everyone could now get back to their normal lives.

"So what's the plan, Boss?" he asked.

"It's simple," Pat replied. "We drop you off in Toronto and then we fly on to Ottawa. You write your report in the next couple of days and send it to me. I'll write mine and both will be sent on to MI6 for their records. And then," she added smiling, "Robert's the name of your father's brother!"

"And you speak to your big boss about moving into the field on a permanent basis." He didn't phrase it as a question.

"That's the plan."

"And if it's a go, what happens to Robin?"

"My parent's will be glad to take him." She chuckled. "That will be the easy part for them."

"That won't be fair."

Pat raised her eyebrows. "Really? To him or my parents?"

"To your parents. I'll take him."

She laughed. "Yeah! So then I have to visit you more often and probably stay the night. You're not even sly about your intentions."

"That would be a positive coincidence I'll concede. But truly, I'd like to look after him. Two lonely old males."

"And when we're on the cruise?"

Ed shrugged. "*Then* your parents could look after him. They live closer to me than to you any way."

Pat thought for a while, chewing her bottom lip. "He's important to me . . ."

Ed interrupted. "Pat, I want to look after him. I wouldn't make the offer out of any intention other than to enjoy his company."

"Okay," Pat agreed. "If I get transferred, he's yours to look after. I'll phone you after I've had my meeting with the boss."

The warning lights were turned on and they returned to their seats for landing in Toronto.

CHAPTER TWENTY TWO

THURSDAY, JUNE 27TH 1985
3 PM

• • • • • • •

"**C**rowe speaking, come fly with me," Ed answered the phone.

"That sounds unlikely," Pat laughed.

"It's a conversation piece."

She laughed louder. "You don't give up, do you? Crowe speaking; conversation piece."

"Hi, Pat. How's it going?"

"Fine, Ed. Can you chat freely."

He stood and closed his office door. "Go ahead."

"Two pieces of news, Ed. One good, one sort of bad."

He was tempted to say 'shoot', but decided not to. "Go ahead, I'm listening."

"I spoke to my boss and I transfer to the field this September. Not sure where, but probably where French is spoken."

"Oh, la, la," he offered. "Expensive coffee on the Champs Elysees perhaps?"

"Or one of many countries in Africa."

"Of course. Congratulations, Pat."

"Next news." She paused. "Our Mr. Griffin is dead. Shot this morning in Dublin."

Ed shook his head. "That is sort of bad."

"It gets worse."

"I'm listening."

"He was shot three times. Once in each leg . . ."

"Oh God, don't tell me!"

". . . and once in his head."

Ed gulped and had to put the phone down to think it through. Pat waited for him to respond. She had thrown-up twenty minutes earlier and knew what Ed was thinking.

He took a deep breath and picked up the phone. "That's unbelievably gory, Pat. But I do want to say something, and I hope you won't get mad at me."

"I won't, because I know what you're going to say."

"I want to thank you again for saving my life, Pat."

"Our lives," she added. "But I do appreciate the comment."

Ed's mouth was dry, and he needed to freshen up his coffee. "Can I give you a call next week, Pat? We can sort out details regarding the cruise and my future room mate."

"Sounds good. Have a beer for me tomorrow night. I'll be thinking of you."

They said good-bye and hung up.

CHAPTER TWENTY THREE

FRIDAY, JUNE 28ᵀᴴ 1985

•••••••

"You're not looking very chipper tonight, young man. Had a bad week?" Karen asked as she poured Ed his first beer. Friday night—The Queen's Head.

"Oh, just a person I sort of knew died. Sudden like."

Karen smiled. "All the more reason to enjoy life, right?"

"True," Ed said, lifting his beer to his lips, "very true." He had been tempted to drop in for a beer after work the day before, but decided not to. Instead he had gone home and started to read, probably for the fourth time, his favourite book, 'To Kill a Mockingbird'. Set in a southern US state, a place he had never seen or read much about, the story of young children experiencing some hard facts of life had always captured his interest. The location didn't seem to matter. It was an experience all children managed to adjust to, all in their own way in their own world. Reading the book comforted him, and last night he had needed comfort. Ordering out for pizza had also helped.

He had decided to limit himself to two beers tonight. He wanted to make a point to himself. He drank his beer slowly, acknowledging people at the bar he knew with a smile and nod. He didn't want to get into a conversation unless he had to.

Karen placed a glass of red wine at the spot next to Ed. "That's a lovely hat, miss," she said, looking over Ed's shoulder. A wave of pleasure washed over him. He smiled but he did not turn. He didn't have to.

"Thank you," Carolyn responded to Karen. She tapped Ed on the shoulder. "Do you like it, Mr. Crowe?"

Ed turned, unable to stop from smiling. He looked at her hat. It was white with a wide brim adorned with red silk roses. "It's very elegant," Ed said, bowing slightly. "I doth see an English rose; and I refer not to the hat."

Carolyn smiled, picking up her glass of wine. She motioned to a table. "Can we chat?"

They moved to a table in a corner. "We can do anything and everything you want us to do," Ed said, sliding his chair close to the table. "I love you, Carolyn."

She reached out and touched his hand. "Yes I know you do, Ed." Her smile slowly disappeared, and she held his hand tight. "I have some bad news, Ed. About us I mean."

The smile disappeared from his face and his stomach hurt. He closed his eyes tightly for several seconds before opening them again, trying his best to smile.

"I can only stay until Tuesday," Carolyn said solemnly. Then she grinned widely, eyes sparkling. "Gotcha didn't I?"

For a moment he was speechless. "Christ, Carolyn, you almost had me in tears there. What did I do to deserve that?"

She squeezed his hand. "Hey, you're the one always playing with words. It is bad news, because I was hoping to stay until Thursday!"

He rolled his eyes. "Okay, you're right. But I've never tried to give you a heart attack!"

She winked. "Why, Mr. Crowe, you make my heart flutter all the time."

He held her hand tighter. "I love you, Miss Andrews, with all my heart. We've got until Tuesday. I'm the happiest guy in the world."

"So I was wondering," she said, closing an eye to think, "if tomorrow we should go downtown Toronto and see a show?"

"Sounds great."

"Or perhaps we should go for a nice drive in the country?"

"That sounds great too."

"Perhaps Niagara-on-the-Lake?"

"Sounds great."

"You're not interested in talking about tomorrow, are you?"

He shook his head.

"You want us to go to your apartment don't you?"

He nodded quickly.

"You want to make me supper, don't you?"

"I've got some cold pizza we could heat up after."

"After? After what?"

He leaned forward; looking around to make sure no one could hear him. "After I slowly undress you; oh so slowly undress you. After lovingly kissing you, and after I have made love to you and made you come twice. Then, and only then, we can have pizza."

"Really?"

"Really!"

"Is it good pizza?"

He narrowed his eyes, giving her a challenging look.

"Okay," she said, finishing her wine. "Let's go!"

Author's Note

This novel is fiction but based, in part, on an actual event.

The Grand Hotel in Brighton, England was bombed by the IRA in an effort to kill members of the British Government of Margaret Thatcher.

Patrick Magee was subsequently found guilty of the bombing and imprisoned. After 14 years in jail he was released in 1999 as part of the the Good Friday Agreement that was signed on April 10th 1998 (Good Friday).